To the Patrons of

Neva Lomason.

I hope you enjoy these
through the years.

Randy Hendrick
Carrollton GA

March 14 2004

The Twelfth Year, and Other Times

The Twelfth Year,

and Other Times

Stories

Randy Hendricks

Mercer University Press
Macon, Georgia

ISBN 0-86554-839-0
MUP/H632

© 2003 Mercer University Press
6316 Peake Road
Macon, Georgia 31210-3960
All rights reserved

First Edition.

∞The paper used in this publication meets the minimum requirements of American National Standard for Information Sciences—Permanence of Paper for Printed Library Materials, ANSI Z39.48-1992.

Library of Congress Cataloging-in-Publication Data
Hendricks, Randy, 1956-
  The twelfth year and other times : stories / Randy
Hendricks.— 1st ed.
    p. cm.
  ISBN 0-86554-839-0 (alk. paper)
  1. Identity (Psychology)—Fiction. 2. Psychological fiction,
American. I. Title.
  PS3608.E54T94 2003
  813'.6—dc21
                                        2003006891

In Memory of

Robert Drake

Table of Contents

The Stove

I

He had not come for the stove. He had come, in fact, just to buy a few goods they needed to see them through until the next trip, sometime in March probably, when he would bring Mary and the girls along. Now they needed shoes for the girls, for they had outgrown the old ones that he had repaired and repaired, and thread and needles Mary had asked for. And then a little something for the girls for Christmas, some candy and maybe some store dolls. And so he had come, starting in the middle of the night, carrying two tow sacks with him, out of the Cove and down the mountain alongside Little River into town.

Now the stove sat at the edge of the plank porch in front of Gray's store; and he sat beside it, dangling his feet over the edge of the porch and eating, slicing thick hunks of cheese from the block he'd bought from Gray and putting them onto crackers before sticking them into his mouth. He chewed each bite absently while staring at the dust piled against the porch below his feet. The flesh below his right eye rippled as he chewed and stared. At one point he completely ignored John Suttles, who twice called his name and then passed on with a grunt. He was thinking of how that morning he had come into Gray's store and greeted the town loafers and the boys that had come down from Chestnut Flats to loaf. And Gray and Mrs. Gray. He had greeted them and told them the girls were stout as bears and Mary was much better now than she had been right after harvest when she'd felt so poorly that folks had sent food in.

Then he had bought the stove.

No.

Then he had seen the stove and remarked on it, and then Gray had sold it to him.

But, no, it was not Gray but something else that had led him to be the possessor of the stove.

And now he sat beside what was undeniably his possession on the porch in front of Gray's store, his possession by some process that was still a mystery to him.

When he finished eating the cheese and crackers, he closed his knife and slid it into his pocket. Then he stood and brushed the crumbs out of the folds of his overalls and watched them fall into the thick dust that had gathered like dry, gray snow against the porch.

He stepped onto the porch and took a piece of rope from the stove's top and began making the strap by which he planned to carry the stove. He tied one end of the rope to one of the stove's legs and slipped the other end though the hole of one of the burners and out again through the fire door. He picked up one of the tow sacks he had carried into town and folded it several times. Then he tied it to the rope to make a pad for his shoulder. He planned to alternate between carrying the stove directly upon his back and carrying it by the rope, thinking that way he would be able to go farther before having to stop and rest. The possibility that he might reach the point at which he could go no farther by either method had occurred to him, but he had laid that by in his mind as he would lay a sack of corn in his bin until it was time to take it to the mill. When he had finished readying the rope, he backed up to the stove, removed his hat, and pulled the rope over his head. With his back and shoulders broad and flat against the stove, he put his hat back on and grasped the inside of the front burner with his fingers. Then leaning forward and pulling the stove, he tilted it until its weight was heavy on his back. Bracing himself carefully with his feet spread evenly, he lifted the stove off the porch. Even with the precaution, the stove's weight almost threw him; and he had to take two quick steps and shift his shoulders rapidly under the stove to keep it upon his back. The shoes and thread, the candy and dolls—the things he had gone back into the store to buy after, in a separate transaction, he had purchased the stove—along with the lengths of stovepipe and the griddles, all slid around inside the stove where he had put them after placing them inside the other tow sack. He had just regained an uneasy balance when a woman spoke to him.

"Where you going with that 'er stove, Mr. Johnson?"

Joby, after some trouble, managed to crook his neck enough to see the woman, Sina Rose Adams, sitting beside her husband Fletcher on a wagon. Through the space below the wagon's seat, he caught sight of the four, or maybe five, children in the wagon's bed.

"I'm taking it home," Joby said.

"You ain't fixin' to carry that thing home, are you?" Fletcher Adams said.

"Yeah," Joby answered.

"Why, lan'," said Sina Rose, "why didn't you bring your wagon to town?"

Fletcher Adams cut his wife a look. Fletcher never grew a beard proper, but Joby could not attest to having seen him when he was within thirty-six hours of his last experience with a razor, and his dark eyes in his dark face gave him a generally menacing appearance. But he was one of the only men who ever married himself out of the moonshine and outlaw climate of Chestnut Flats into the respectable community of the Cove; and he was a good enough neighbor, though he sometimes recalled too avidly or too fondly certain exploits of some of the Flats folks he had lived among. He was immune to the disapproval himself, but it embarrassed his wife and her family, one of the oldest in the Cove.

Joby answered Sina Rose Adams as pleasantly as he could under the weight of the stove. "Well, now, ma'am," he said, and then he grunted and shifted the stove, "if I'd brought my wagon I'd a had to push it. I ain't got no mule right now. Yeller Kate up and died about two weeks ago. The cancer, according to Miles Thompson. And I'd done sold Half-a-Ear John. I been borrying a mule for this and that from Henry McCulloch since."

"Joby, I don't see why you didn't borry to come into town," said Fletcher. "Especially hauling something like that heavy step-stove. Why, that thang must weigh 200 pound."

"Well, now," Joby said, and his eyes brightened even as he grunted and panted under the shifting weight of the stove, "I didn't know I's going to be hauling this thing when I come. I figgered on giving McCulloch's mules some rest. I was only figgering on taking two tow sacks back up the mountain when I went."

"Well, why don't you leave it 'til you get a wagon to haul it?" Fletcher asked. "Or wait a couple or three hours and we'll take you back as fur as our place anyhow."

"I reckon it's mine to tote now," Joby said. Then he stopped talking as if no more talk was needed or even possible, and with a nod, he turned, his feet seeming to screw down into the earth, and started walking along the road out of town toward the river.

Both Sina Rose and Fletcher knew, as everyone knew, of the inordinate and legendary strength of Joby Johnson, who had once lifted a man up and pinned him against the ceiling of a room and held him there sprawling until the man admitted he had drunk Joby's whiskey without first being invited. Fletcher Adams had seen it. But that had been a long time ago.

Still sitting on the wagon seat, Sina Rose murmured, "It ain't ever man could do it."

Fletcher looked at her for a moment; then he looked back up the road at the step-stove that was walking off on Joby Johnson's thick legs. "It ain't ever man *would* do it, neither," he said. "Asides, he ain't done it yet."

II

By the time he reached the river again, where he had planned to first ease the stove's weight from his back to carry it by the rope, Joby had already made the change three times. He had not been careful enough the first time and the slipping weight had jerked him backward so hard he thought for a moment he had done some real damage to himself. When he realized he was all right, he began to imagine having to lie down there on the road and wait for someone to come along and see him beside the stove, broke-down and a confirmed fool. He thought about that picture for a long time, even after he was on his way again. He even imagined someone coming and bending over him and brushing his sweaty black hair out of his eyes. He imagined saying to this stranger, "I reckon I'm a confirmed fool." The stranger did not say anything. He just kept doing things to help the poor man lying there poured out like water. "I always been real stout," he imagined saying to the stranger, "especially for a reglar-sized man. And it ain't just me says so." Then he thought how if it really happened it would not be a stranger who stopped but someone he knew, because he knew everyone who might come along this road, at least by sight; and by blood or marriage he was some kin to a right smart of them.

So by the time he actually got to the river, he had concluded he would have to take his first rest there. He backed up to a sweet-gum tree and sat down slowly, letting the stove shave the bark off the tree all the way down to the root. When he had gotten himself out of his makeshift harness, he took from his overalls bib pocket some papers, matches, and a sack of tobacco he had bought from Gray—considerably crushed now by the pressure of the rope against his chest—and rolled a cigarette.

The river was quiet there where the road joined it. The ford was further upriver. In the summer townspeople came to this spot to swim, but it was deserted now. Joby still wouldn't look under his collar to see the mark he knew the rope had made on his shoulder, despite the tow sack he used for padding. He looked steadily at the river instead and smoked. Then he raised his eyes and admired the good stand of trees growing up the rise on the opposite side of the river. There was a loose vine that hung from its entanglement in the high limbs that the town boys had cut for swinging out over the river. He picked out a good canoe tree, although he hadn't made a dugout since he was thirteen years old. Then he remembered those woods belonged to Talbot, who was Gray's kin.

Son of a bitch, he thought, but he immediately suffered a powerful inward tremor and felt humbled for having thought it. It was the kind of thing he would have thought about a man in the old days. Before he found Jesus…and Mary. Or really the other way around. It was the kind of thought he would have had in the days when he would come from the Cove and Gray would come from town and Fletcher Adams wouldn't have to come from far at all since he was already planted in those parts, and they might all be sitting around the same table at that house in

Chesnutt Flats talking big and drinking whiskey and smoking and chewing and sometimes fighting. It was funny how he and Gray and Fletcher Adams had all come out of that alive and now were something completely different from what they had been.

Then he remembered how that morning coming into town had been like it always was, how he had greeted the men and Mrs. Gray as he always did, how he had told them all that the girls were as stout as bears and that Mary was much better than she had been back just after the harvest when she'd gotten so sick and people sent the food. Then he had sat around and smoked and talked, his foot the whole time set upon the two tow sacks he had laid on the floor as though they might crawl off. One of the town men was a one-armed man that had fought for the Confederacy, but there were Union men there, too, and some whose families had tried to be neutral. They talked of the war as if they had fought it just a month ago, except for the absence of fear and the hard feeling. And when he saw his chance, Joby reminded them of how his father had seen his own brother murdered by North Carolina bushwhackers who were raiding the Cove for food and horses and anything else they saw and decided they wanted. And guerillas had sometimes taken the food directly from the families' tables. Many of the stories were so bad that they had become a kind of standard to measure modern problems by. Joby, born twelve years after the war, sometimes looked at the survivors and thought they didn't seem to measure up to the stories people told about it. They ought to look different, it looked like, but they didn't.

That morning, the stove was sitting in a nook between two shelves behind the long counter Mrs. Gray used to measure material for the women. On top of the stove was a wooden crate overflowing with different-colored scraps of material. Joby was wondering what Mrs. Gray might ask for the crate of scraps when he'd discovered the stove under it.

"What you asking for that stove?" he wondered out loud.

Gray got up from the chair he occupied most of the time and walked over to the stove. "I'll have to get eleven dollars for this thing," he said as he took the crate of yard good scraps off the stove and set it down on Mrs. Gray's counter. Joby got up and walked toward the stove, remembering to pick up his sacks.

He was then suddenly conscious of the fact that his interest in the stove, an accident of wandering thought, had centered the interest of the store. All the others now shifted their bodies and turned their heads, even changed their breathing, and looked at him and Gray and the stove. It all made Joby feel awkward, and he had nothing more to say.

"Eleven dollars, you say?" he said anyway.

"Yeah," Gray said firmly, not frowning, but Gray had a way of insulting the Covites who came into his store without coming right out and doing it. And the one thing he would talk about until the day he died was his father's having seen General Sherman near Knoxville while the older Gray was still driving a sutler's wagon. Gray liked to recall his father's impression, "You'd think the old cuss would look like George Washington or God a'mighty, but he looked like a shriveled up hillbilly rotting on his own corn." Gray had been talking about Sherman since the days when he would come up from town and Joby would come down from the Cove to Chestnut Flats to sit in that house and drink. And he never failed to put a lot of emphasis on the word *hillbilly*.

Joby did not look at Gray. He stood at the end of the counter gripping the two tow sacks in one of his broad hands and staring directly at the stove's front. There was an embossed name on the stove's door: SAFEHEARTH. And below the name, BOSTON, MASS.

"I reckon that's a fair price," Joby said.

Behind him someone chortled, signaling another general shifting of postures and chuckling that streamed up to Joby's back and stopped.

Then he'd bought the stove.

No.

Then he'd said to himself, eighteen dollars and thirty-eight cents, the sum of money in his pockets, all that was left from the corn he had sold to Thompson for Thompson to sell again in Knoxville and from all the firewood he'd loaded and hauled into town to sell over the late summer and the early fall and from selling Half-a-Ear John.

Then he'd said to Gray, "I reckon I'll take it off your hands."

That had brought on another chortle, but no chuckling. He felt another collective shifting of bodies behind him, but he was more aware of Gray, whose forehead got smaller, as a man's will when he's calculating close.

Joby took his wallet from his overalls bib and removed some folded bills from it. He carefully separated the bills and laid them upon Mrs. Gray's counter. Gray picked up the stack of money and folded it. Joby watched the bills go inside Gray's pocket. Then he watched Gray's hand come out of the pocket again, empty. Gray was grinning at him. "You must have robbed the bank on your way here this morning," he said.

Joby fought down something that was rising up in him then and said, "Will you help me get it outside?"

"Sure," Gray had said, still grinning. Gray was ten years older than Joby, a tall man, straight in his back, and with thinner arms than any other man in the room. They were thinner even than his wife's arms. Mrs. Gray's forearms and wrists were thick from years of milking before she became Old Becham's wife, and the long sleeves she wore didn't hide their thickness, the cuffs pinching the flesh. When Old Becham died, Gray married her and took over Old Becham's store.

Now by the river Joby believed that what had been rising in him was a flame of hatred at Gray for being Gray, for being the uppity town man with a fat wife, for being all that in spite of the time they'd spent with Fletcher Adams and others like themselves down in Chestnut Flats. Hated him because he'd courted Mary before he left her to marry Old Becham's wife and left Mary.... Well, no, he hadn't left Mary ruined because things hadn't gone that far. But along with Joby's hatred had risen the knowledge that he was a fool and that he needed to separate out all this feeling from what he was doing and just say, "No, I reckon I better not take it this trip, after all." But he wouldn't say it.

So now he possessed the stove.

It sat there by the tree next to him. To buy it he'd spent the money they had held out for winter. They would have had enough, and he still had his tobacco crop to sell, but he had to buy at least one mule from Thompson before spring....

"Dang it," he suddenly said to himself, "Mary needs a stove." He felt better then, and he wished he'd looked at it that way sooner, but the gratification wore off quickly and he had to convict himself all over again because he couldn't make himself believe that he would have bought the stove just for Mary if things hadn't gotten the way they'd been. It was not simply that he couldn't bear for the men in the store to think he was poor. They all knew he was what he was, just as they knew themselves to be no different. No one in those parts except Thompson and Gray had ever had much, though he personally had more than he'd had in his life since Mary's father had deeded to him the land he had worked since he was seventeen years old. But Mary's sickness and the dead mule made him uneasy. And he had sometimes sat outside in the evenings and just wondered if it

was still possible for a man to lose everything, really to lose
everything. Even more than the way his father had lost food off
the table and shoats and apples to bushwhackers during the war.
More like the way the Bible's Job lost everything and the
Egyptians got boils. Buying the stove was a way of stacking
things up against the door against all that, but the effect had
already worn off.

And he'd bought it because of Gray, because of the way
Gray made a man feel. Handing over that money to Gray was
like reaching across a table to pour whiskey out of a demijohn
into his glass in that house in Chestnut Flats. Because pouring
whiskey for a man, whiskey you had paid for, could be more
than a friendly gesture. It could be a sign, practically a statement,
that you held the other man to be no better than you. But it was
wrong to look at a man that way, and he was ashamed of himself
for doing it, both with the whiskey in the bygone times and with
the money that very morning. Because if you really held the man
to be no better than you, there would be no need to pour the
whiskey or hand over the money.

But he still possessed the stove.

III

In the house there was a rich yellow light. Mary was sitting in
her chair by the fireplace, a cavernous opening with dark walls.
The heap of ashes told of an even larger fire earlier in the
evening. She always made the fire too big when she built it
herself because she was cold natured. The children lay soaked in
sweat under thick covers on the bed in the corner behind their
mother's chair. But tonight the big fire had been more than the
result of habit or her nature. It had been a kind of protection
against the fear that rose in her as she sat waiting for Joby while
the hour grew late.

When the door did at last open, Mary sat forward suddenly and then stopped at the edge of her chair, as if something had caught her. She looked up at the dark figure in the doorway, knowing it was her husband by its shape, but recognizing, too, that the figure was somehow misshapen. "Joby," she said. "Joby, what...?"

Then she came to him and put her hand upon his shoulder and left it there as they walked together to the fire and he sat down. He walked bent over, and slowly. When he had eased himself into a chair, he told her in a few words what had happened, in a voice weak and raspy from his heavy struggle. The one thing he did not tell her was that he was sure someone had followed him back up the mountain, and he eyed—only once—the shotgun standing in its place in the corner. When he had finished, she brought him a plate of beans and salt pork and boiled potatoes. He ate a little of the food and finished the coffee.

"I reckon if a body waited 'til he thought he could afford a thing, some people might never get nothing," Mary said.

Joby nodded, sat silently, not eating the food now. His legs trembled violently as if the muscles craved the labor they had grown used to. It occurred to him that it must be very late at night.

Either because he was too tired or because he had half expected it, he did not move immediately when the banging at the door began, even though it was insistent. Finally, Joby got up and moved toward the door, frowning at the stiffness and pain. His shoulders pressed upward against some phantom weight. He picked up the shotgun as automatically as he would his hat to go out into the fields in the daytime.

When he opened the door, he saw John Gray, who was just about to bang upon it again. Gray's face was twisted and small, and in the dim light it sat impishly on the tall man's body. Next to him, but a bit farther back in the dark, was Fletcher Adams.

"Come in, fellars," said Joby, putting the gun back in its place. Except for the weariness that reached even to his throat, it might have been three o'clock in the afternoon the way he said it.

Gray hesitated for a second, but, casting a sidewise glance at Fletcher, he came on in. Fletcher came in, too, and moved past Gray, who had stopped just inside the door. Adams walked quickly across the room to the fire and began to warm himself.

"Nobody taken sick?" Mary asked as Joby closed the door. "Did youns come from my mother's?"

"No, ma'am," Fletcher said, "ain't nothing like that."

"Well, have you men had any supper?" she offered. "Or I guess it's nigh time I was cooking some breakfast."

"No, we won't be staying for a meal," Gray answered sharply. "Thank you," he added, the way he might speak to a woman customer in his store.

He and Fletcher Adams exchanged a quick look. Gray turned to Joby, who was still standing by the door he had just closed. "I come about that business we transacted earlier today," Gray said. "I can't be party to a family doing without in the cold coming on. I brought you back your money."

He pulled the bills from his coat pocket and laid them on the table. They were the same bills Joby had paid him for the stove, and they were folded in the same order. Gray put them down on the table and seemed to press them as if he would put them even farther down before he withdrew his hand.

Joby watched him, and as Gray's hand was withdrawing, Joby's eyes remained fixed on the money for a moment. Something was rising in him again, like swelling. He didn't know what to say, or rather didn't know that he really did know, but then he was saying it.

"I believe we made a concluded deal, John Gray. I'm obliged for your concern, but I reckon I'm responsible for my family's keep." Whatever was swelling inside Joby was breaking up as he spoke, as if the words, or some words, had the power to break up whatever might swell up in a man.

"Damn it, man," Gray said, "I ain't interested in your responsibilities."

"I can't allow such talk in my house," Joby said.

Fletcher's head rose a little higher out of his shoulders. Mary stood by her chair where she had stood since the men had come in. She didn't seem to move at all. Not even to breathe.

Gray was hard all over and his face trembled. Joby instinctively dropped his right foot back to brace himself and shifted his taut, sore upper body forward. He blinked as Gray moved, but then he saw that Gray meant only to get out. Gray opened the door and passed quickly through, leaving it open behind him. Joby, after a moment, closed the door, and turning back toward the fireplace, he discovered that Mary was holding the iron poker in her hand, pointing it like a saber at Fletcher, who had not moved and who was not taking his eyes off Mary's poker.

"I hain't got nothing to do with this," Fletcher said, holding up both his hands to shield himself.

"Mama," said one of the little girls from her bed in the dark corner, but none of the adults looked that way.

"No, ma'am," Fletcher went on, "I ain't come for no trouble."

"I ain't understanding this," Joby said, stepping toward Fletcher. Fletcher leaned slightly toward Joby, but he didn't take his eyes off Mary and he didn't lower his hands.

"Ain't no call for that poker, Mary," Joby said.

Mary lowered the poker, slowly, but she did not stop watching Fletcher, and she did not back away.

Fletcher lowered his hands and cautiously turned toward Joby.

"Joby, I ain't got no quarrel," he said.

Joby nodded.

"I just come as a witness." Fletcher turned back toward Mary appealingly. The poker dropped a bit further, until its tip touched the floor.

"What he said ain't the truth," Fletcher began. "He made it up standing there. He couldn't brang hisself to tell you the real truth. He come because he got hisself in a knot he had to come to get hisself out of. That's why he come. When me and Sina Rose went in the store after we seen you, he was a standin' up there talking to them fellers 'ats always in there seems like…. Well, he was sayin' some things I wouldn't want said again. And then he finally said, 'If'n he,' meaning you, 'carries that thing all the way home, I'll give it to him.'"

"Give it to me?" Joby said.

"That's right. Everbody set up and took a new interest then, and Gray looked like ants had done crawled up his britches legs cause he knowed he'd said the wrong thing. Them Chestnut Flats boys don't hold no notion of a man's word at all unless it's a makin' some kind of a bet, but let a man wager something like that and they're for bringing out the Bible and they'll hold him to it or ruin him, and Gray knowed it.

"He started to trying to beg out by sayin' they wasn't no way to verify it now, but somebody said 'Hell, he,' meanin' you, 'could be gone after.' Excuse me, but that's what somebody said. And Gray grinned and said he couldn't do that cause he had a store to mind. Then Mrs. Gray come through and said, 'Mind what? A bunch of loafers?' One or two of the boys got a mad look at that, but most of them just cackled like Mrs. Gray had done them a good turn, and you could tell they wasn't going to lose interest nor let the thing drop 'spite Gray's excuses."

"God-almighty," Joby said, almost whispering, "give it to me."

"Yessir. And I don't know what come over me. It was like we was all a gang of boys hanging a cat or something. I up and said I'll go with you, and that sort of seemed to settle the whole thing. Sina Rose pinched me on the arm, but I'd done said I'd go, so I told her to finish her business and drive on back to our place. And they was a few more bets made fer and agin you and more being made when me and Gray set out after you."

Hanging a cat, Joby thought. *I was the cat.*

"We follered you all the way here, hanging back and being quiet."

But I made myself the cat, Joby thought.

"That was easy enough, least 'til it got dark. You know I'm a pretty good hand in the woods, and Gray wasn't anxious fer you to know what we was doing. When we come up on you settin' by the river, Gray figgered he had it made then. He said, 'By Ned, he ain't made it more'n this far,' and I said, 'You never said nothing about him not stoppin' to rest.' He looked at me like he was fixin' to quarrel, but he knowed he was in the wrong and a store full of witnesses. So we set down and waited fer you to get going again. It sounds awful sneakin' like now, don't it? But it seemed all right then. Like it wasn't really sneakin', not mean sneakin' anyhow."

The word *witnesses* hung on in Joby's mind, suspended from all the others Fletcher was saying. *I knew they were there. I knew....*

"But I'll have to say I never figgered you'd make it either. You looked so tuckered out settin' there. And when the grade steepened, you could hear old Gray's breathing started sounding like he couldn't keep the laughing out of it 'cause neither one of us considered you'd get that stove up again after you set it down another time.

"That was the doggedest thing I ever seen how you figgered a smart way to rest. You ought to of seen him, Mrs. Johnson, leaning that stove back against them trees so he could take some of the weight off'n him without a settin' it down. And a standin' there agin it, taking your rest. A man don't stiffen up so bad that a way, does he? A man could do better by going on with some little chore while taking his breaks. That's why I usually shell a little corn or something while we're resting from putting up hay or something. Them boys will say, 'Why don't you light and rest a spell, Fletcher,' and I'll say, "'Cause I don't aim to stiffen up,' and they'll shake their heads, but dreckly when they move they'll moan and catch theirselves and I'll laugh at 'em for not believing me. And that's like what you was doing by resting agin them trees. He must of stopped four or five times, Mrs. Johnson."

Joby moved to the table and sat down on the bench. By talking, Fletcher was bringing back to Joby's mind what exhaustion had already put out of it, leaving only his muscle to remember the weight of the stove and the half ease of leaning back against the trees. But it had not been a smart thing.

Desperate was the word Joby thought. *He ain't telling it right. It wasn't like he's saying.*

Fletcher now stood more relaxed before the fire. He even coupled his hands behind his back and spread his feet wider, as he naturally would any other time he happened to stop to warm himself before their fire and naturally take the chance to tell a yarn. Mary still stood with the poker in her hand, its tip on the floor.

"But that last time you stopped you looked done fer. We couldn't see you much, though we could still tell where you was by sighting yours and the stove's shadders. We could just hear your breathing mostly, which was sounding like you was choking, on blood we figgered, and we started to come, but then you hawked up and spit and your breathing got easier. Gray said that didn't matter. He was going on to you anyway. He said he wasn't going to stand by and let no man die. But I seen. I told him, no, he wasn't going to go and rob you. And in a little while you was moving agin, and we knowed you was close enough to home that you'd make it now.

"When you went in the house, we argid a spell. Gray says he wasn't going into no man's home at this time of night, but I said we was here and knowed you wasn't in the bed and they wasn't no real good reason not to go on in and take care of his business. And he knowed, I could tell, that he couldn't get out of it. They'd be more crow than he could ever swaller if'n he went back without coming on in. But, by dang, you seen him. He couldn't brang hisself to tell the truth oncet he was here. You seen how he was, all eat up cause he had to lower hisself. Course Gray hates to let any money out of his hands, but it was the pure shame more."

"You mean he's shamed of having to bring it to us," Mary said. She squatted now before the fire and used the poker to stir the embers under the only remaining log on the dog irons, not bothering to ask Fletcher to move aside. Simply assuming he would. And he did, and Joby thought, *It is over for her now. She has put it away, in that way she has.* Her face, sallow still from her illness, looked golden in the glow of the fire. She didn't look up from the embers she stirred, and neither of the men said anything in answer to her. *What is she really thinking about an old beau who did that? Who came to her house and put dirt in it?* Joby wondered, but he would say nothing to her about that. He looked at the bills lying on the table where Gray had left them. *They don't mean anything. But she has put it away, just like the sickness.*

Fletcher moved toward the door. "I'm a going to slip on home now. Sina Rose is probably got twenty or thirty of her male kin looking fer me by now."

Before he opened the door, he turned to look at them. "Mrs. Johnson," he said, "it ain't ever man would carry home a stove like Joby done today."

Mary did not look up from the fire. "I know it," she said.

Joby rose from his bench to shut the door after Fletcher.

"Night to you," Fletcher said to him. "I reckon you know folks will be talking about you. I can't wait to hear Gray's version."

"Goodnight, Fletcher," Joby said, and he watched Fletcher Adams stride off across the front porch and into the dark. Then he closed the door.

Mary had risen from stirring the fire and discovered the two girls sitting on the side of their bed together with their skinny white legs hanging over and their bare toes pointing down, those of the bigger girl almost touching the floor.

"Get to bed now," Mary said, and the girls rolled over and scooted themselves under the blankets.

Joby moved slowly from the door to his usual chair by the fire. The log on the dog irons broke in the middle, sending ashes rolling forward over the hearth and sparks fluttering up the chimney. Mary put two logs on the fire and stirred and banked the embers beneath them.

"I knowed they was there," Joby said.

"Well, of course you did," said Mary.

"I was afraid for a while that it was some of them Chestnut Flats boys going to get them a stove."

"You can find plenty of Chestnut Flats boys willing to knock you on the head," Mary said, "but you won't find many willing to tote nothing as heavy as that stove very fur." She paused. "You might of killed yourself, Joby Johnson."

"I know it. I knowed it at the time. But it seemed like I didn't have good sense to know what I knowed."

He stretched his thick legs before him and examined them. "I won't be fit for much for days to come," he said. "I'm a fool. If Gray had just told me to my face he'd give me the stove if I toted it home, it'd all be different."

"But he didn't," Mary said. She stopped stirring the fire and stood up.

"Yeah, I know. That 'baccer will be in case in the morning. I'll pack some of it down before I start."

"I'll help you oncet the girls get fed and off. Don't want you to get too late a start."

Joby Johnson stretched himself again and smiled at his wife. He was spent, and it was a pleasure to take his ease. He could feel himself drifting off into a warm sleep.

Mary smiled back at him, and then turned to the fire again.

Joby came awake again and sat up. "After that I'm going to slip across your daddy's bottom over to the Adams place," he said. "See about borrying Fletcher's mules. I been borrying too much from Henry, but if I can I aim to make that thing a whole lot lighter going down than it was coming up."

Ruins

One summer night during the early '70s I was sitting on the front porch of the old home place with my grandfather. We'd been listening, independently and silently, to a single cricket chirruping somewhere close by. Then all of a sudden my grandfather spoke to me, startled me I was so intent on the cricket's noise there in the dark. He said, "Johnny, when I was in Florida before they shipped me overseas, I saw a man reach into a oyster he'd just pulled out of the ocean and he took a pearl from it. Prettiest thing I ever seen. And it come from that ugly little rock critter. I asked that fellar as fished it out how he reckoned a oyster made that thing and he said there ain't no reckoning to it. Said that a speck of dirt got in the oyster and the irritation caused the pearl to make. You think about that. When something gets inside a man like that, he has a heart attack or a cancer or he murders his children. But the oyster makes a pearl. Now which one is the world fit for?"

"The oyster," I said, because I didn't know that the question was rhetorical; but he didn't hear me—or he at least made out like he didn't hear me. And then my grandfather said to me,

"Boy, that hair of yourn is getting kind of long, ain't it? You ain't turning into one of them hippies, are you?"

I didn't think he was crazy then. I still don't think he was crazy, maybe. But the next night he sat alone on the porch and shot himself in the head with his Remington single-shot .22. He had carefully scrawled a suicide note apologizing to my grandmother.

But this is only a memory I have of my grandfather, one of many that I attach to a string of scenes fashioned from the memories of others to form a pronoun: *him*. I do not know my grandfather's story. I am therefore compelled to tell it.

And I will begin with the place. To get there, you drive along the river road going north out of Williamsville. The last time I was there, sometime in the late '70s, the land was covered with milkweed, sawbriar, and scrub pine, all of which had grown since the clearing for the reservoir well over a decade earlier. For nearly twenty years the reservoir had been delayed first by one barrier and then another in the game of public domain, manifest destiny, suit and countersuit, breaking out of legal channels into occasional brawls and a few instances of rifle fire. There wasn't much grass under the scraggly growth, just an occasional clump of sedge, thistle, or weeds for which I didn't even know the names. Most of the ground under the ragged growth was exposed red clay sliced up with an intricate maze of narrow ditches.

I stopped once on the way to take a look at a spot important to my boyhood. It was a spot below a ridge where the land sloped sharply down to the river. From the top of the hill to the water's edge there was nothing but flaky red soil and a few jutting white-gray rocks. The narrow ditches running through the earth behind them widened and deepened as they cut through the slope and wound around the boulders on their intersecting paths to the river.

When I was a boy that descent had been covered with grass and trees, and down close to the river there had been about twenty feet or so where the land leveled off and there were two giant cedars standing together, so big you could sit on their roots out over the river and stay dry even in a heavy rain, a natural canopied pier. I fished there all the time. Sometimes we'd come here, my friends and I, and build a fire and fish all night. I came with my father and Uncle Charlie and Uncle Lem a lot, too. And even my grandmother liked to fish with us. She loved to eat fish better than anything.

But that was a long time ago, and I could not separate the land as it appeared the day I last went back in the late '70s from all that had happened before when I was a boy, and even before I was anything at all. By that time, late in the decade, my father was in the real estate business and the local real estate economy was depressed, though by some calculations it should have been in the third or fourth year of a boom. He was holding his own, though he worried much and spent a lot of cuss words on a variety of fools.

Even that late in the game, with the land cleared, most folks moved, and the dam constructed, Preacher Sharp at the Baptist Church was still referring to the US Government as the Devil, and he had not always been alone. My father, in fact, had said some of the same things early on about the reservoir, but he had gradually shifted sides as his own dream shifted from being a farmer to another kind of dream that even now is fuzzy to me. And when he had dreamed of being a farmer, a big farmer, I mean, he, like all the other farmers, had never believed the promise that the reservoir would improve the quality of life for us all. He would have been a natural ally of Preacher Sharp, who saw the argument with Old Testament clarity. But my father, as I said, had changed. He had been a grocery clerk and a mechanic and a used-car salesman and a surveyor and now a realtor aligned with the side of progress and planning, and he was not without influence in the community. Through all this he had become one of those rare and not always admirable people, a curmudgeon saint of all experience, widowed almost as long as he had been father to a son who confused but never defeated him, willing, in fact, to take all his son's attachments—with the exception I am trying to tell about here—in such rough grace and love as he was prepared to give. Never saying yes when he meant no. Never scared to say no. And sometimes hell no.

So in a way the reservoir conflict, at least a few years earlier in my childhood and on into adolescence, had seemed simply a conflict between Preacher Sharp and Daddy. Looking back, I think it's probably wrong to even talk about opposite sides when there were so many sides, so many angles to approach it from that you can't really tell who squared off against whom.

But any chance any of us had to see the complexities at the time dissolved when the marine biologists from U.T. discovered the snail darter in the Little Tennessee River and the lawyers evoked the Endangered Species Act to stop the dam. All this occurred after the dam was built and the land had been scraped clean and all but one holdout, Jack Tanner, had not only moved out of the houses they'd lived in for years, and in some cases their parents and grandparents and way on back had lived in before them, but any semblance of house, barn, well, or outdoor toilet had been razed, shaved off like stubble. Then, if it wasn't right on the river, only fruit trees or rose beds or tame blackberries were left to suggest that anything taller than a groundhog had ever inhabited the place. And those like my father cursed the government for its stupidity while Preacher Sharp indicated, as much as a preacher in a fairly big church could without being carried out in a straightjacket, that Providence had intervened. And suddenly Williamsville and its dilemma were reported by no less than Walter Cronkite, and we saw our restaurants and barbershops on the evening news and felt strangely important. Men in overalls defied the occult Ph.D.s who claimed that the tiny fish was a newly discovered species with the counterclaim that the damn little pollywog swam in virtually every branch they had ever waded; they'd seen them. Well, it wasn't the first time we'd defied science and foddered the media in our parts.

And all the while Jack Tanner was the image of that defiance, an implacable and fierce defiance on the threshold of violence. He sat on his porch waiting, some said, for the opportunity to shoot anyone brave or fool enough to set foot on his property. Of course there had been more like him in the beginning, but they had worn away over the two decades until he was very much alone now in his defiance. But the marshals would come for him the next week. I had heard that already on my visit in the late '70s. For the snail darter had been successfully transplanted to other streams and the reservoir was going forward, so the battle was nearly over, the battle, I mean, between the little man and the government which we stage so well here in the South, where historically, with our poverty and ignorance and the dirty faces of our children and bare feet of our womenfolk, we've been a right convenient source for those in the television and picture magazine trade.

But I fall too easily into the wrong tone. An easy mistake and a diversion.

So back to the place. Not far beyond the spot where I had fished as a boy, you turned from the river road onto a much narrower one, the bed of which was made up mainly of loose dirt and deep ruts and paved by old leaves that stick before they can get blown into the shallow ditches. There were thick woods on both sides of the road, because here you were beyond the clearing. And though they really had nothing but the woods to hold back, barbed-wire fences ran on both sides, their strands thickened with rust, collapsed and entangled after the slow decay of wooden posts and the one-by-one expunging of staples. The rotted posts stood more on a flimsy principle of balance than on any density of their own, supported in addition by the stubborn, vine-like refusal of the wire to relinquish its hold so the posts could lie down to a decent death.

Then you came to the clearing. My grandparents' place. The road passed through woods again before emerging at the top of a hill where the ground was level. The grass that day grew tall and brown around a square patch of dirt where nothing but stickweeds grew. Two red maples stood purposelessly symmetrical on either side of a walk of flat stone, barely visible in the tall grass, leading to where the house once stood, ending at two concrete steps that led up to an emphatic absence.

The house that had stood there seems larger in my memory than it must have really been. It was a two-story house, though, so it loomed large even if it didn't spread out much. It was plain and usually in need of paint, but my grandmother always had the yard fixed up nicely with flowers, even if she did set them in beds she made inside old tractor tires or rusted out washtubs. The barn and the hog lot had been across the road from the house; the garden was out back and to the left of where the house stood.

Long ago it had no doubt been a place with a sleepy, bucolic beauty. But its story, if it has one, has a bitter ending, as I indicated at the start. That's all there is, all I have experienced personally of the defiance, though my grandfather did not fight the TVA like Jack Tanner. That kind of thing was against his nature. He wasn't a pacifist; he was just introverted. If that's the word. Maybe he was just perverse. My grandfather never fought anyone as far as I know after World War I when he came home from Europe and bought the land. At first he built just a small house with only a couple of rooms in which he lived with my grandmother and then for a while with Uncle Charlie and even

Uncle Lowell while he built the big square two-story house nearby. He did the work largely by himself, except for some of my grandmother's cousins and some of the neighbors pitching in on the heavier parts. He cut the timber alone and used a mule to snake the logs out of the woods and then a team to haul the logs into Williamsville to the sawmill on a flatbed wagon. Then hauled the boards and framing lumber back out there again to cure. He built the house around the demands of the farm and working all day Saturdays at the sawmill, at first to pay for getting his lumber sawed, then for cash. So it took him nearly five years to finish.

On the night they finally moved into the house, my grandfather pushed himself back from the supper table and said to my grandmother, "By god, missy, you got you a house as good as the Williamses now." My grandmother would tell that on him years later as though it were very funny. I never thought it was, but of course I didn't know. Naturally it wasn't true. It was just a big square clapboard farmhouse one step up from a shotgun in its design. And there were even Williamses still living in the old mansion then, so the comparison was really silly. But my grandfather was ready to burst with pride, I reckon. And with good reason. It makes me think about him differently than I probably would otherwise, after all that was going to happen happened.

So they lived there and had four more sons and a daughter—my Uncle Lem, who survived; another boy who didn't; my Aunt Venis, who was married twice and divorced twice and spent years telling all the women who come into her beauty parlor that she would never marry again until she finally did; my father; and finally, my Uncle Jeff, who, though the youngest, grew up to become the first to leave home for good and as far as we know is right now somewhere in the world serving as a ship's cook.

But that's not part of this story. Or, yes, it is. This story really starts, I suppose, during the Depression, which was a very interesting time for the effects it had on the family. There is a politician in this story, Franklin Delano Roosevelt, who was elected President of the United States something just under fifty times, and he did two things better than most people. One was talk in a way that made you believe he was your smartest friend and the other was to pick men. He surrounded himself with talented, high-minded men who must have all thought they had stepped into the pages of a fairy tale. The old rules did not apply, the times were enchanted, and these high-minded men could do anything they wanted, just about; the ogres and the giants couldn't touch them. One of the things these high-minded men and Mr. Roosevelt did was establish the Tennessee Valley Authority. They did this to save the South, of course, as high-minded men have been wont to do for a good many years now. So, Mr. Roosevelt and his band of high-minded men brought the dark South into the light—literally, if not figuratively.

No, wait. I'm being sarcastic again, and that's the wrong tone. Because good did come from it all, honest and tangible good. Flood control and electricity and some good jobs to pay for the electricity. I heard my grandfather say many times, sitting at his kitchen table under the bright, bare electric light that you turned on by pulling a string that hung from it, or in the dark at night on his front porch where he liked to sit in the evenings, that Franklin Roosevelt had been a good president. My grandfather never got emotional about politics. In fact, the first time he ever voted was for Roosevelt and then only when he was running for a third term. I suppose he was keeping a close watch the first two terms to decide whether this one might turn out to be worth the trouble of a special trip into Williamsville.

See, my grandfather had a longstanding disgust with government stretching back to the war, which is perhaps when this story really begins. He never talked about it much during the years I knew him, even though I believe he talked to me more than to anyone else during his last years, but somehow I have learned that he was opposed to the war on some unarticulated grounds, for reasons formed during or after the war, because he would not have had a politics in the common sense before the war, just a cautious patriotism that would make him leave my grandmother voluntarily a few months after they were married and go away. He left her with the Walkers, her parents, with whom they were still living when the war came. And even after the war he still wouldn't have been able to align himself with any party.

Let me back up. You may be wondering how I know what my grandfather felt about the war, since he never talked about it much. You may be assuming that he discussed these things with my father who in turn passed them on to me. That's not the case, though. No, I know these things about my grandfather by some method of transference more mysterious than a simple telling. This knowledge somehow just washed over me, but it is as real and indelible somehow as the one thing my grandfather did tell my father long after the war and what my father, in turn, told me, on a strange, warm night, as if he'd been saving it, turning it over and over in his mind like he would a gold watch in his pocket, and then giving it to me that night like a man taking an heirloom out of his pocket to hand over to the heir.

He said that in Belgium my grandfather had been in a patrol that had captured six Germans in a communications bunker. They had taken their prisoners back to a small dugout bunker of their own where the Germans were interrogated by a lieutenant from Muncie, Indiana, a violent little man, apparently. When the prisoners, evidently a pretty run-down and ragged-looking group, refused to answer any questions, the lieutenant ordered a sergeant who in turn ordered my grandfather, my grandfather simply because he was the first private the sergeant's eyes fell on in the blind luck of military lottery, to shoot a particular German soldier, who was chosen with the same lottery blindness. My grandfather did it, evidently without so much as blinking. And as he raised his rifle and fixed the sight somewhere on the forehead, the prisoner's face, which looked to be about forty or so and had a thin three-day growth that made him look like a haggard hill farmer more than anything like the pride of his homeland, suddenly became alive with terror as he realized what was about to happen. Right then my grandfather fired the shot that froze the German's face in a hideous expression that remained in death, until it was somewhat obscured by the blood from the head wound covering his eyes and filling his gaping mouth and overflowing like a fountain over his bristled cheeks. A fine shot, of course, in the tradition of Alvin York.

Well, maybe I am adding things and getting ironic again. Over the years it's become a picture in my own mind and what's in that picture, I guess, is what I am telling more than just repeating the words my father said that night when I was a boy. And he probably was doing the same coloring and adding that night himself.

But this part is certain. My grandfather told my father, who, like me, was a boy when he first heard this story, that he never again wanted to be somebody that just did what somebody else said without thinking. When the sergeant gave the order, there was no chance of its not being carried out, because in a place like that it was easy and maybe even necessary to give up yourself and become nothing but the function at the end of another man's voice.

Yes, of course, he did only what he had to do. That is the old defense we fall back on. But I don't think my grandfather ever completely convinced himself of that, judging from what he told my father about it. It was just too easy for him to do it. And

I think it all had something to do with my grandfather's coming here to this secluded place to build his home after the war. There must have been a reason why out of all the muck of that ugly war it was this incident that he told.

The story of how my grandfather got to be himself again after the war is the story I don't know. I don't know how any soldier does it, or if any ever truly do. But it was after he was home again with my grandmother and building this place. He put aside all connection with the larger world, as least as much as it was possible. That is, until Franklin Delano Roosevelt and his high-minded men had sufficiently proven themselves for him to straddle his mule that fall and ride to Williamsville to mark his ballot.

But mostly he was just there, in that place, with my grandmother and the children, whom I cannot even imagine as children. And they just worked. I can barely imagine any of them before 1941. Uncle Charlie, Uncle Lem, and Uncle Lowell were all in World War II, but the war ended for Lowell at Normandy, and so did any hope of his ever walking straight again. Aunt Venis was the next oldest child and she worked for a coffee company in Knoxville during the last three years of the war. My father, though, was only eight in 1941, and so it was all a spectacle for him. And he explained it all, no doubt, for my Uncle Jeff, who was three years younger. And probably with all the stupendous inaccuracy with which the very young instruct each other about war, sex, and anything else romantic, mysterious, or important. I know how the two of them must have felt about the war because I had my own war when I was a kid. They would have killed Germans and Japanese in the woods around their house, just as I and my cousins killed Viet Cong around ours, in glorious anticipation of the day it would all be real. But we all missed our war. I suppose I should thank God.

Anyway there was a lot more talk about my uncles' war when I was growing up than about my grandfather's war. Very little of it about the actual fighting, though. In fact, I'm not sure any of it was about the fighting. Growing up I heard stories about poker games and fistfights, and there is a particularly pathetic story about Uncle Lem and a buddy of his driving a jeep all over the roads of a Philippine village trying to catch up with what a brief glimpse had confirmed as the "the cutest little set of nipples a man ever saw on a slanty-eyed gal." There was quite a bit of this kind of talk when I was growing up—around the barn, of course, never around the house. And there was a lot of drinking that went with the talk, again, though, only around the barn. And that kind of talk and the drinking didn't even go on in the barn when my grandfather was around. When it was time for cutting hay or tobacco, my father would bring me, for years just to watch, until finally there was the glorious conversion from what had seemed an interminable childhood and I joined in the work.

By that time, when I was little, I mean, before I helped with the work, my grandfather was coming to the fields or the barn for only an hour or so at a time—to tell them how to hang the tobacco or to tell them they were stacking too much hay on the wagon—and then he would go back to the front porch and watch from a distance, and maybe one of my aunts would bring him a jelly glass of iced tea to drink while he sat there. And in the barn or the lean-to shed, after the hay had been stacked, or the corn put in the crib, or the tobacco hung, in the afternoon, after they'd eaten the big dinner the women had spent the morning cooking and the rest periods were coming more frequently, they would sit, Uncle Charlie and Lem and Lowell and my father and sometimes Uncle Jeff if he happened to be home at the time and maybe a neighbor or two—they would sit on the wagon bed, on the threshold of a stable door or the door of the tack room, and they would pass around that jar with the mercurial brew hot as mule piss (as they said; I wouldn't know that myself until later), and they would talk.

The talk would not be bawdy then. That would be more likely if I was alone with Uncle Charlie or Uncle Lem. But the talk would be of people they all knew and things they had done growing up. And each one of them already knew everything that was ever said at those times, and they would nod and grin as they took turns in the talk, each knowing what was coming next, speaking and listening less to tell or learn something than to confirm something, perhaps affirm something to themselves, something larger than the little detail they were going over at the time, something that demanded a voice different from their normal voices, a voice more thoughtful, even in laughter, than the voices they spoke with to make aluminum or sell insurance or tune up a car.

Then later, I must have been a teenager and I'm sure I had noticed it by then, though I hadn't yet said it to myself, my grandfather was an outcast from them. By all that was right he should have been there in the barn or in the field with them, reaping the gain of the sons he had sown. But he was at best an archaic and superfluous figurehead sitting on the front porch day by day as we passed by on the wagon on our way out to the field or back to the barn, never so much as nodding, not even seeming to see us. And his sons and his son-in-law, the one that stuck around awhile, seemed to see him no more than you see the lawn statue you've walked past every day for twenty years.

But I saw him because I had access to the talk of both worlds at the farm, the circular talk of my father and uncles in the barn and the linear talk of my grandfather on the porch. Their day talk and his night talk. And I was overhearing both. Well, there were really three worlds, because there was the world of my grandmother, who spoke history and poetry to me in the mornings as she stirred gravy on the stove top. Though it would be many years before I would realize that what she spoke was history and poetry. I do not mean the history and poetry of books but that which lived in her mind and flesh. But it is another story I have started to tell here.

My grandfather talked sometimes on the porch at night about when he was a boy over in West Tennessee. Life wasn't good. His Pap, as he called him, had beat him pretty badly a few times before he—and he was only eleven—skedaddled for Arkansas with some woman, not as an adoptee but in some kind of unspoken contract that called for her to feed and house him until he reached the manhood necessary to provide her with whatever it was she wanted, needed, or expected from the deal. I've always gathered it didn't take him long to provide that, though no grandfather, not even one who could be as perverse as mine, would name exactly what that was to a grandson. Then when he was fifteen he came walking back home again and found his Ma and his sister and his sister's new husband on the farm and Pap gone, having fallen in with a woman himself and left for parts unknown. All Grandpa knew was that he hadn't met them on the road from Arkansas. Grandpa would just laugh when he talked about the old codger, as if he meant no more to him than some water moccasin you might see already downstream from you, and swimming away.

As I look back, I see I just referred to him as my grandpa instead of grandfather, as I have been saying all along. I note the fact not to explain it, because I can't explain it, but I will let it stand in case it proves meaningful.

Sometimes he'd start talking about the second war there on the porch at night, though never his own. He talked a lot about Lowell, especially, whose ruined knee and missing thigh parts were less the cause of paternal anguish than some sort of symbol for my grandfather, and he would talk about the Emperor, Il

Duce, and the Fuehrer, not calling them that, of course, as if they had personally surrounded Uncle Lowell to inflict the wound.

If he wasn't talking about any of those things, he would tell me stories about hunting after he and his Ma had left the farm to the sister and her husband and come to these parts, where his Ma's family was from. About the bear and the deer and hogs he killed. He never went hunting when I knew him. He said there was no game anymore except on preserves, and he said that was a chicken shit way to hunt. He was referring to the fact that my father and my uncles and I, too, sometimes drove over to Crossville for a weekend hunt on a private game reserve. But then my father told me if I kept listening to my grandfather eventually he would tell me about the time the house was surrounded by Indians.

But he only talked about these things when he and I were alone, or maybe when some of the other grandchildren were there; he didn't talk to the grownups anymore, at least not the way he talked to us. Or really talked at us, or maybe just gave that impression while he was really talking over our heads and might have been doing the talking even if we hadn't been there. For all any of us would do would be to listen; it was seldom the kind of talk you talked back to, any more than you would answer the preacher in the pulpit, not even to shout a good old Baptist amen, in this case. But at some point I began to connect things. Like when he'd talk about Lowell I'd remember seeing Uncle Lowell gingerly creeping down from the tractor seat, because driving was all he could do, and I would think about what was missing under his pants' leg. And then I noticed that he took the longest drinks when they passed the jar around.

And then sometimes at night, Grandpa would sit on the porch in unbroken silence. And the silence would become so heavy that we grandchildren would eventually shuffle off the porch out into the yard for our own night games and night talk.

I just remembered something funny. My grandfather bought a wild boar one day and brought it home and put it in a stall he built especially for it in the lean-to attached to the barn.

Why? That's the sixty-four-dollar question. And, God, what an argument! I remember being in my grandmother's kitchen one morning—it must have been the day after my grandfather and Jim Ray Peters brought the hog in, built the stall in the lean-to, and unloaded the hog without saying anything to my grandmother or any of the others about it. And I remember my father, who on that day for the first time I began to see as being separate from the rest of them, because after my mother died they were all just my family and he was pretty much indistinguishable from the rest of them up to then. But now I began to see that he was younger and louder than the rest of them. He was saying, "What in God's name were you thinking?" Saying that to my grandfather. I was scared to death. They were all so mad they didn't think about my being in the room. And Uncle Lowell, who was the only one sitting besides my grandfather, and Uncle Lem and even Uncle Charlie, although all more quietly than my father, were saying he was crazy if he thought they were going to hang any tobacco over that thing. And how much did he pay for it anyway? It was some ridiculous price, I reckon. I don't recall just what. And what if one of the grandyoungons got in with it? My grandfather just sat there quietly and took it all, took all that from his children, as if they owned the place and he was a wayward son. He never through the whole thing took his eyes off the tin salt and pepper shakers in the middle of the kitchen table.

And the boys kept on, because it was a conundrum that raised the same points over and over again and they were all just too befuddled to get beyond asking those questions. Until finally my grandmother said, "Hush, it's done done now." And if

Hecuba had said it just that way the poor women of defeated Troy would have stopped wailing.

I wish sometimes I had done what I wanted to do that day. Though it is crazy. I wanted to say, "Leave him alone." Sometimes I even came so close to saying it that the words were like a bad taste in my mouth, like the aftertaste you can get from belching. Of course, if I had said it, all hell would have broken loose with its contents aimed at me; but sometimes I play the whole thing back in my mind, only this time I do say it and leave them standing there gaping as my grandfather and I walk out of the room together. It wouldn't have happened like that really, but I wish I'd said it just the same. I don't have very many moments like that in my past, moments when I stood for something.

Standing for something isn't right, though. Maybe it's just standing period that I'm thinking of. Sometimes I wonder if my grandfather was not really just sitting and taking the abuse, as it appeared he was, not the way you normally think of people doing something like that anyway. Maybe he was standing then, not for anything, just for himself. Maybe he was not just a crazy weak old man. Maybe he was sitting there being himself; and, thinking that, I know if I had spoken out then, he would have only looked at me and we would not have left the room together—which is not to say that he would not have admired me and even loved me for it—it's just that leaving the room like that would be too Hollywood for anything my grandfather ever did. And I am so Hollywood I have to wonder sometimes if I didn't actually invent at some later point in time the desire to act that I have come to believe I felt on that day.

What if he didn't react to them that day because he was above reacting to them, if that makes sense? I know that the boar did stay, perhaps simply as a reminder to my grandfather of the wilderness he had known in the first decades of the century, and Uncle Lem and my father did hang tobacco over it, even though my grandfather told them not to. They did it as if they had to be as defiant as he, a curse in the blood. They did it for three years in a row. And once while they were climbing the poles over the boar's stall, Uncle Lem said, "If I fall in there, John, I want your leg to pull myself back out again." And my father said, "Then you better grab it on the way down." That was the funny thing I remembered.

Maybe they weren't defiant just because of blood, but because they hated him so much by then. If it was hatred. And his obstinacy might well have deserved hatred. They say my grandfather used to go through the cornfield after the boys had thinned it and thin it again, thinning it too much. He did lots of things like that just to make them feel small. At least that was the effect, whatever he intended. He wouldn't put running water in the house for years and years for no reason anybody could fathom, and my father and his brothers saw this as a deliberate way to add misery to my grandmother's life. One Sunday morning after my Aunt Venis had gotten ready for church, she being the only member of the family who went to church, he made her stay home and blacken a stove instead. I know all these things happened, but I can't say that I ever saw anything like this in the years I knew him. By the time I came along, things had kind of reversed.

I should probably rethink all this. It's just so damned hard to get it right, to talk about it and make any sense of it, to get the words right, and the attitude. If I'm not sounding like a sarcastic ass, I talk as though I'm swimming in some Faulknerian amniotic fluid and haven't taken the first breath on my own yet.

Because you see, he couldn't have really been that different. He did things the way normal people do, too. He bought a new red Farmall tractor in 1951, and a decade later he bought a two-year-old Chevrolet pickup, also red. He never drove either one of them a lick himself, but he bought them for the boys to use. They took him and my grandmother to town on Saturdays in the truck, and, of course, they ran around in it themselves as young hellers.

I remember one day as I sat on the front porch of my grandparents' house, fall, a pretty chilly day, a Saturday no doubt, I saw that red Chevrolet coming up the hill toward the house with Uncle Charlie driving and my grandfather standing up in the bed alongside something big. I wondered what in the world he was bringing home this time. This had to be the year after he had gone out to the barn one day with the Remington .22 single shot and stuck the barrel through the boards of the boar's stall and shot it. And then he burned the carcass. He did all that as silently as he had bought the damn thing in the first place, only now three years later there was just a general throwing up of hands in the family at the things he did.

Naturally this act drew comment from all the neighbors. About the state of mind he must be in to do a thing like that. But he was oblivious to anything anybody thought. At least, that's the way it looked sometimes.

It was an electric range he had in the back of the truck. He and Uncle Charlie carried it into my grandmother's kitchen where there was not even an outlet for it. Then they both sat at the kitchen table for a while drinking coffee and admiring it. My grandmother had been to the barn to gather eggs, which is odd to remember because I should have been doing that for her; and when she came into the kitchen, she stopped and stared at the bright, white range for a minute. I know what it was. I had been sick that morning. I wasn't supposed to be on the porch at all but in the living room where my grandmother had built a fire, maybe the first of the season. That's right. I'd gone out because, to tell you the truth, I was sometimes scared to be in that house alone. When I was little they kept me from climbing the stairs by telling me Red Eyes and Bloody Bones lived at the top. And I could see those two phantoms as clearly as I could see any of the people.

And so, even later, a big boy in junior high, I always felt uneasy if I was in the house alone.

Well, there was no change in her expression really when she looked at the range. She didn't look surprised or sour or sullen or anything you might expect, just slack-jawed, the way she always looked except for now and then when she smiled at something and her cheeks rose like blankets being lifted from a bed to get the folds out.

"Where'd you get that?" she finally said. It wasn't the first thing my grandfather expected her to say, I reckon, because it took him a second or two to say he had gotten it at Heritage Furniture.

"Well, what did you get it for?" was my grandmother's next question. She hadn't taken another step into the room. She just stood there holding that tin pail of eggs and staring at the stove and asking questions.

"I got it for you to cook on," my grandfather said. Then he told her she was getting too old to be building a fire every time she started to cook something, and it was true that she had been going downhill some the past couple of years.

"Getting too old, my ass," my grandmother said. Then she moved. She walked across the kitchen carrying the maybe a dozen eggs in her pail and set it down on the table, but only a little more firmly than she did every day when I handed her the eggs and she set them there before she separated them into the ones she would keep and the ones she would sell. "I don't reckon I been complaining about building no fires," she said. "Been building 'em all my life."

"That's just what I meant," my grandfather said. "And these daddang wires are running through the house for some use."

"There ain't even a place to plug it up," my grandmother said.

"They can be," he said. And the next week there was. So the electric range sat on one side of the large kitchen and the wood stove on the other, and from then until the time she had to move, my grandmother got up every morning and built a fire in the wood stove to warm the kitchen before she cooked breakfast on the range. Except summers, of course.

All the boys and Aunt Venis, too, were glad my grandfather had bought the range—what they really said was that it was about time—and they all said my grandmother's initial resistance was only because she was set in her ways almost as bad as he was. But my grandmother was not set in her ways. She could learn to live with anything.

Like the baby who died, and Uncle Lowell, who died in 1970, of pneumonia, they said. When you stop to think, there's been quite a bit of hardship in her life. When you go back over it you see the peaks and the valleys. Growing up with it, it was all just them, but when you think about their lives you see the tragedy. I always got the feeling that for her it was all just one long, level plain, that my grandmother never believed life could be better than it was. Not fundamentally. She had no conception that life was dull or hard because she was married to my grandfather or anything so causal as that. And so I came to think that she was beaten by it, by my grandfather, the farm, the children, beaten until she became that image, the opposite of Melanie Wilkes, the shapeless, thin-haired, toothless hill woman with bad grammar. But she had some talents. She could live with my grandfather and all her children and not alienate any of them. She could stand the boar and the electric range on her own terms.

But I never saw that until just this moment. I reckon all I ever saw was the defeat. I certainly never saw the talent as I got older, into high school, my life changing as I grew to be a pretty good football player, which could transform your life in our parts. I started to hate what was there at my grandparents' place.

It stank of warm cow's milk and slop jars and cold ashes. I saw they were ignorant and I was ashamed of them. Most of all I just couldn't stand to be around people who were that god-forsaken dull, trapped in a static round of nothing for which they seemed too stubborn or too ignorant or too something to do anything about, even to recognize. Of course, that's just how young people feel, but even when I was older, college age, and looked back it was painful to realize that the people who had loved me most in the world were like that. And it certainly never bothered me that not once in the four years of high school did my grandparents come to watch me play football. My father always went by their house on Saturday morning, and he would tell them all about Friday night's game, and I reckon they would listen because when I would come by later in the day, as I always dutifully did to make sure they had firewood and to do whatever other chores needed doing, they might mention something about it. But my father's trying to get them to come to a game was like trying to get them to go to Africa. Both were places they had no business.

There is a part of me that argues against all I am saying. If they were happy there... No, not happy, but content maybe, why shouldn't they just stay there and be what I call dull? They stayed together, didn't they? Doesn't that say something for them?

But, you see, it would never have occurred to them to be anything other than together. You would never even think of the word *happy* when you looked at them, any sooner than you would think of the word *rich*, not even as opposites of what they were. Because you would not ever think *unhappy* or *poor* either. You would just think *them*.

I'm only now getting to the part that I thought was the whole story when I started.

One day as my grandfather was walking back to the house from a far meadow on his property, he came upon some men. Surveyors. Two months later, he got a letter informing him that his land was being taken for the reservoir. At first he was just incredulous, like he was when people started talking about going to the moon, or when he'd talked to the polite men doing the surveying that day and they wanted to know if he actually hadn't heard about the dam. That was after he had gone up to them to ask why they were surveying so far from the river.

He said they were nice enough fellows, but I've always suspected they were condescending. And that might have had something to do with the fact that he did not believe at first that it was going to happen. My grandfather had never swallowed the argument that regional redevelopment would improve the lot of the valley dwellers by increasing the land's appeal to investors, industrialists, and small businesses. "I thought they just wanted to generate some more 'lectricity," my grandfather said. "I'd a been all for that. But this other don't make sense. How come somebody else has got more right to the land than I do just cause he's something 'sides a farmer?"

He wasn't the only one around here who asked that question. My grandfather's incredulity, however, never turned into the rank cynicism that, in time, you could see in the others. In fact, soon everything, even incredulity, seemed to be gone from him, and he was very different. Whenever we'd visit, he'd be sitting on his porch, like a sentinel, though watching for God knows what. And he never talked about the TVA or losing his farm. He talked a lot about Franklin Roosevelt, though, and things that happened when the boys were growing up, and about his baby son that died, and sometimes he'd talk about my mother and how good a woman she'd been, but he wouldn't talk about her much if my grandmother was nearby because my grandmother wouldn't let him. She'd use my being around as an excuse to hush him up, like even at sixteen I didn't have any business hearing about my mother. But the real reason was that my grandmother just couldn't stand to hear it herself. My mother and my grandmother were very close, I have gathered, and I know that my grandmother nursed my mother through her last illness until her lungs gave out altogether because of the CF.

Then there was the night my grandfather talked about the oyster and complained about my hair. And the next day he shot himself. When my father and I arrived that night, there were other men there already along with the ambulance crew who took my grandfather's body away. One of the men showed my father the note my grandfather had written (my grandmother had been taken inside by some of the neighbor women), and my father read it. Then he dropped it and turned around, and as he walked by me I heard him say, "The goddamned son of a bitch." I'd never heard anything before, or since either, that frightened me as much as those words, and as far as I know my father has never seen cause to regret them.

I picked up the note and later I gave it back to my grandmother, but not before I saw that the note said that he, my grandfather, could not bear to see her in her condition, which I assumed meant the condition of about to be out of a home. My grandmother stuck the note inside her family Bible, right there with all the other information about births and marriages and the more natural deaths in our family. The note is still in the Bible and the Bible is locked up in a cabinet in my father's house along with some small things that belonged to my mother and some other things my grandmother left him. I don't think my father ever looks at any of that stuff.

There is one more thing I should tell you. Before my grandfather's funeral, during the receiving of friends, which was of course in the house there, my grandmother and I stood over his casket together. She took my arm in her bony little hand and said, "He brought me a box of candy one day when we was courting, and he told me he knowed he wanted me since the first time he laid eyes on me."

And that did it. I broke down right there in front of all those people and I cried. I cried so hard that my poor little grandmother finally had to hold me up. I cried for him and for her and for me. Him the stubborn and perverse old man whose first twenty years were filled with venal and martial adventure that he turned off like a faucet for the next forty and at the same time seemed to turn off any way to have a fruitful connection to his children. Her the small thin shapeless woman forever stirring something on a stove, fired or electric. I had always seen them as just two people who lived on cornbread and pungent cow's milk and too many onions, people that I was forced to love in a respectful and dutiful way that was not sufficient to overcome the shame. And it had always seemed to me that they were bound together only by some agreement about the place they belonged to, something that afforded both of them some dominion in some old-fashioned rule of order. I had never suspected that there had ever been between them something as intangible and risky as passion. My god, my grandparents had loved each other.

It wasn't until after the funeral that my grandmother told us that the "condition" my grandfather referred to in his suicide note was actually a malignant tumor in her left breast. So he had left her alone to face that, and she faced it and lived at a time before it was common to survive such conditions. So you see my grandfather's gesture was not such a clear one. Not really a defiance of the TVA or anything like that. Maybe he could have stood one of the things, the cancer or losing the place, but both together were too much for him. Or maybe it was everything, from his Pap's beatings to the adventures in Arkansas on down to remembering the oyster on the porch that night. Everything all lined up like knots in a rope. Or maybe it was the failure of his gambit after the war. He had made a truce with the world in which he agreed to withdraw to his place and make no more demands in exchange for the privilege of not being a function at the end of the world's voice. Had he himself broken that truce by saddling the mule and riding into Williamsville that day to cast his ballot? Perhaps his life can be viewed as tragic if you see his suicide as his last way to hold on to the kinds of things he'd settled on that hill for in the first place. But whether or not you see it as cowardly or stoical depends on how Roman you are in your point of view, I reckon. I know my father is not very Roman.

That time in the late '70s I'd come back to visit my father and my grandmother, the survivor, living in her new house in town (she would live to be nearly 100 and die quietly at last in a nursing home). And I had seen over the few days I was there some old friends, morphed out of their overalled hillbilly status by the grace of Sam Walton's dream, and their children were actually the second generation who could smile for their school pictures because they saw a dentist regularly, and they all had visions of speedboats and jet skis.

One evening during that visit I sat in my grandmother's new living room watching the CBS Evening News with Walter Cronkite. My grandmother, still the one to feed and serve whoever came into her house, was bringing tea in from the kitchen. Then the report came on. I watched as the camera angle shifted from the familiar on-the-scene reporter to the familiar house—the medium-sized white clapboard house with its black shutters and navy gray porch floor—certifying, I thought, the reality of a place I'd seen with my own eyes all my life, but at the same time raising it, or reducing it, to a new, competing reality. The camera followed the marshals getting out of their Buick and walking up to the front steps. Then the shot switched to a perspective from inside the house and caught the broad-chested officers coming across the porch. Jack Tanner leaned on the doorpost just inside the screened door and watched them coming. One of the marshals said, "Mr. Tanner?"

"Yes, sir," Jack Tanner said.

"Mr. Tanner, I expect you know why we're here."

"Yes, sir, I reckon I do."

"Are you ready to go?"

"Yes, sir, I expect I am."

But Jack Tanner kept leaning against the doorpost, not looking at the first marshal who had come inside, nor at the second marshal who remained on the porch, but through the screen, apparently at something in the yard. His body looked small in that leaning position, his head was slightly bowed. Then he turned back toward the marshal in the house, and even in the poor light the camera caught something of the creases in his face and the round monkey eyes. He spewed air over his trembling lips. "Hell of a country, ain't it?" he said. In the next shot, one of the marshals was helping him into the back seat of the Buick.

My grandmother was saying, "Here's your tea, honey." But I couldn't turn to face her. I was afraid the heavy water gathered along my lower eyelids, the dams holding everything back, would overflow.

The Peddler

"It beats the sawmill."

This is what Carl Peeler thought as he drove the ten-ton paneled truck over the rough back roads that had been scraped through the knob country east of Williamsville.

It was hot in the truck. Nearly August now. But he remembered it had been hotter rolling logs up ramps to the sawyer and loading boards on trucks and trailers at the other end of the line. This was better.

At the sawmill, though, there had at least always been someone to talk to, even if some days it was down to just old man Eckersley operating the conveyer lever with the one arm he had left while he laughed at his own jokes that no one else could hear until he remembered to shut off the saw. It was a pretty long ride between houses in the peddling truck, especially on this Thursday run through the red knobs, and when you got to the houses, like as not you had to wait for somebody to happen back from the barn or field, and some of them when they got there didn't have more than five words to say, as if living out away from folks that way they'd just lost words, like the trout in the dark underground lake cave in the Lost Sea had lost their eyes because they were never in the light anyway. It was all pretty hard on a naturally social man like himself.

So he'd taken to pulling out his Jew's harp when he pulled up to a house and nobody in sight. He liked to pass the time that way, and it was good for calling somebody back to the house, for they'd most always notice the strange twanging there in the still afternoon and come on.

And he pulled it out now as he stopped right in the road at the path to the Bowers place, even though he'd seen through the clearing a ways back all four of them dirty but good-natured Bowers children sitting on the porch waiting for him. Well, good-natured even if they was a little stunted and on the funny-acting side of normal. So he got out of the truck and played the Jew's harp and waited for them to come out of the bushes and into the road, which they did. Then came Mrs. Bowers behind them.

"Howdy, ma'am," Carl said to Mrs. Bowers, taking the Jew's harp away from his mouth. "How youns this week?"

"Oh, we're fine, I reckon," Mrs. Bowers said.

"Needing some things I expect."

"We got to have some more lard and flour. I declare I don't know what we'd do if you run on Fridays 'stead of Thursdays."

Poor Mrs. Bowers wasn't too bright a woman. But then you didn't have to be all that smart if you lived here in the knobs and all you ever made was bread and babies. Carl grinned at his own thought and congratulated himself on living where he did. His own wife was going to have a baby.

Now came the best part. As he reached up to unlock the door to the paneled truck bed, he kept his own eyes on the faces of the two littlest Bowers children. Lord, they had dirty faces. It did look like she'd wash them sometime or teach them how to wash themselves. Water plentiful in the knobs and free at that.

Sure enough both faces were frozen on where the door would be open in a second. But then so were the second two faces, and so was Mrs. Bowers's face for that matter.

So Carl went ahead and opened the door, and then he saw it, the little eyes all coming alive and lighting up at the sight. There tacked to the inside of the door was the two foot by three foot advertisement for Merita bread with the color embossed picture of the Lone Ranger, flying across the plain on Silver, though there was just most of Silver's head and back in the picture, and even the Lone Ranger didn't have legs because they seeped right down into a loaf of bread. But plenty of him showed—his white hat and black mask and red neckerchief and blue shirt and black gun belt, and he held his smoking gun out in front of him like he was shooting a bandit riding ahead of him. Carl Peeler had to admit the picture was still quite an eye grabber even for him, but for these knob people week after week, why you'd a thought he'd brought the movie theater out from town. Or maybe they thought the Lone Ranger really was going to ride right out of the picture and ride them all around the knobs on Silver.

Carl climbed into the truck and came out again carrying the twenty-pound sack of flour over his shoulder and gripping the handle of the five-gallon can of lard. He jumped from the truck to the ground, landing smooth and grinning at his own spryness. A thought was forming, but he replaced it by thinking of his pregnant wife.

He set the lard and flour on the ground, and the two older children dutifully claimed one each and started back on the path toward the house. Mrs. Bowers was handing him two dollars and fifty-seven cents, like she'd spent the whole day doing nothing but waiting to buy the lard and flour off him. Two dollars and fifty-seven cents was what the lard and flour had cost the last time she bought some from him, but today it cost a nickel more because prices had gone up. If he told her that, though, he'd have to wait while she went back to the house for another nickel, and that would take as much production as starting a new crop. Or she'd shout to one of the older children to bring one back, which would be worse. Plus it was just hard to disappoint people who worked that hard for something so simple.

"Mr. Johnson says groceries is going up," he said. "Says that was what the wholesalers tell him anyhow. You might ought to bring a little extra with you next time, just in case."

"All right, then."

Mrs. Bowers turned and started up the path but the children stood still. They wouldn't budge until the glory of the Lone Ranger had been sealed away from them for another week.

On impulse Carl went back into the truck and got a quart of chocolate milk out of the refrigerator that he himself had figured out how to run in the back of the truck. "Here, youngons, you take this. And share it."

He had to pick up one of the children's hands to put the treat in it. Neither of them reached for it. They seemed as stunned as if the Lone Ranger really had ridden right out of the picture.

Mrs. Bowers had turned back around. "Mr. Peeler, I didn't bring no money for that."

"No, ma'am. No charge. This is just Mr. Johnson's and my way of saying thanks to good customers."

"Well, thank you kindly."

The children had stopped looking at the quart of chocolate milk and started staring at the picture again. Carl closed the door to the paneled truck, then squatted down before the children.

"Now here's what you do," he said. "You get your mama to pour this into a pan and heat it up for you. Then when you drank it, you think 'I'm a dranking cocoa.' You don't call it chocolate milk, now. If you call it cocoa, it'll taste a lot better to you. All right?"

"All right," one of the children said. But neither one of them changed expression, except maybe they looked a little more scared and water-eyed.

"Come on youngons," Mrs. Bowers said. "We got to get on back to the house."

As they walked away, Carl, on another impulse, pulled out his Jew's harp again and played them back toward home. He sure was in a strange mood today. But he reckoned he should only have to pay for half that chocolate milk because it was a good idea to do things like that for customers and Henry Johnson could just pay his half. But he'd make up the whole nickel on the lard and flour himself because that had been his doing.

It was over a mile then to get to the next house, the last one on the Thursday run. The Woods place was at the back of the knobs, not too far from the paved road he always took back to the store to keep from backtracking over the rough ones. He'd been thinking about this last stop all day. And he suddenly understood why he'd given the chocolate milk to the Bowers children.

Little Jack Woods, a sullen fourteen-year-old boy who already had a man's face and looked all the more queer for it because he wasn't a very big boy, was stretched out in the front porch swing. It was a big front porch, and it was a big house for the knobs. And the inside was different from the other knob houses too because Big Jack Woods worked away from home on construction jobs, so they had money to buy nice furniture, even a color television, which seemed like a waste since the reception there was so bad.

As Carl came up to the house, Pauline Woods came out. She was wearing a brown housedress and had her hair pulled back and pinned. She didn't have on any shoes. She was wiping her hands on a dish towel.

"Little Jack, it's time you went to milk," she said.

"Why, shit fire. Nanny ain't even thought about walking out of the bottom and back up towards the barn yet."

"Then I reckon you better go down to the bottom and get her."

"What for? When she'll be here on her own when it gets milking time."

"Milking time is when I say it is. And I said it's time."

The boy threw his short legs out of the swing and the rest of him seemed to just follow them without will into the house. He came right back out again with the milk pail and stomped by Carl without even looking up at him.

"It's hot," Pauline said. "Come in and have a cold drank."

Carl made sure the boy was far enough away. "There ain't going to be none of that today, Pauline. I can't do it."

"Can't do what? You telling me you can't drank no more? Or be sociable?"

"No, I drank," Carl said, feeling his resolve breaking. "Yeah, thank you, I'll have a cold drank."

He followed her into the house. The front room was dark and cooler, but they went on to the back of the house, to the kitchen, and it was warmer there. She poured two tall glasses of iced tea and handed him one. He took a gulping drink.

"What are you so nervous about today, Carl?"

He knew it was time now. "I just can't be with you no more, Pauline. Betty. Betty and her expecting and everything. I got to think about my family."

Pauline said nothing. She kept looking at him with her dark eyes unchanging.

"Lordy, it's too hot to breathe in here," she said at last. She put down her tea and reached behind her head to take out a pin. Her long brown hair fell around her face and over her shoulders like a closing curtain. Holding the pins in her mouth, she ran her fingers through her hair several times and then she pinned it back again.

Then she looked back at Carl. "Do you expect me to cry now?"

"No," he said. But he really didn't know what he expected.

"I don't think I'll be crying for the likes of you."

"No, I reckon you wouldn't."

She kept looking at him, her eyes hard, like glass. Harder than glass, to judge from the sweating glass she'd just put down.

"How is Betty? It's hard being swoll up in this kind of weather."

"She's holding out."

Pauline used both hands to fan her skirts. "Hard on anybody right now," she said.

She raised her hip to the edge of the kitchen table and pulled her dress above her knees. Carl Peeler stared at the brown flesh of her legs. Pauline Woods sunbathed and people talked about her for it. She was ten years older than Carl.

"So you've come to virtue, have you?"

"No, it's just that it ain't right to do what we been doing."

She laughed at him. "What exactly is your definition of virtue, Carl?"

"What we do—it's, it's just absurd."

"Absurd? My god, have you ever even used that word before in your whole life?"

Carl Peeler couldn't remember that he had ever used the word before. It was as though the world suddenly demanded a new word out of him.

"I'll tell you what's absurd, Carl. Being stuck here day after day with a sulky, half-idiot boy and nothing to do but be hot."

Then she got up.

"You don't mean what you say, Carl. You love me. You said so, and you ain't the man to say what you don't mean."

She was opening her dress as she came to him.

By the time he got to the creek bottom, Little Jack Woods had stopped being angry about having to go a full hour or more before milking time to get the cow that would have naturally come to the barn on her own anyway when it was really time. He wasn't even thinking about what he knew Carl Peeler and his mama were doing back up there in the house. His mama was a whore. So what? They was all whores anyway. When she wadn't laying out naked in the sun she was under that bastard. Or maybe on top of him like he'd seen in that book his cousin had showed him. That bastard coming around in his goddamn big truck like he was hot shit. And before him there was that Homer Brakebull that come around to do thangs his daddy had asked him to. Goddamn 'em both.

Nanny was knee-deep in the creek and not too interested in getting out again. *I might a knowed*, he thought. He picked up a stick and started down the bank. "Get on out a here, you goddamn hussy!" he shouted. But then, goddamnit, he was sitting down in the creek bawling, and Nanny was looking at him.

Little Jack actually liked milking; he always had. He liked how warm the milk was. And he could feed the barn cat several feet away straight from the tit. But he'd never felt like he felt as he milked Nanny straight into the creek and watched the thick white milk thin out and stream down the brown water. He milked her dry. And then he headed back. He knew what he was going to do.

When it was over Carl just lay there in his sweat and thought over and over again that it was all absurd. But he knew as they lay together what it was that made him come back again and again and what had broken his determination this time. It

was the sounds she made, and the way she said his name. Betty
was just still and grunted a little when he laid with her. When
Pauline said his name and made those sounds, it was like he was
home. Maybe that way of loving was just something women
learned over time. And Betty was still just too young to have
learned it. But he was young, too, and by God he was going to
quit being so absurd. Even if it meant he had to give up the
peddling truck and go back to the sawmill. Hadn't old Eckersley
told him he was the best hand he'd ever had and to come on back
any time he wanted a job?

"You'd better go," Pauline said. "Little Jack will be back
any minute. He's a hand for dodging work anyhow."

When he got to the door, Carl turned and said, somewhat
uselessly, "This will be the last time."

"Whatever you say," Pauline said.

He felt heavy and tired and more absurd than ever as he
walked back to the truck until he noticed the door of the truck
was standing open and the Lone Ranger was riding there like
he'd burst out. "Damn careless," he thought at first, but he didn't
remember opening the door. Then he saw the padlock, broken,
no, cut, and on the ground. "Son of a bitch," he said, but
aimlessly.

Carl Peeler didn't think about Little Jack until about a half
second before the boy was standing there in the door high above
him with money bulging in his pocket and three or four Merita
honey buns in his hand. He was also holding a pair of long-
handled metal cutters, which he brought down hard on Carl's
head. Carl couldn't see, but he could hear Little Jack's nervous
squealing laughter as he leaped to the ground and he could hear
him running away.

Carl realized he was on his back, and about the only thing
he could feel was blood, he guessed, oozing through his hair and
behind his ears. Then he could see. He was looking up at the

Lone Ranger. "Shoot him, you son of a bitch," he said. He thought he said it out loud, and then he said, "God, what's wrong with me." Then he just said, "Oh, God." Suddenly he could see the Lone Ranger very clearly, clearer than real, shining, brave, absolute in his perfection, there above him, where he belonged, against the sky.

Things were changing. The sky was fading. Silver had run off, and now the Lone Ranger sat astride a loaf of Merita bread, which was reared on its end like a horse on its hind legs. The Lone Ranger was pointing his gun toward the fading sky, and, like some wild masked god, was laughing down at Carl Peeler, who was lying there on the ground and thinking who in hell would drink hot chocolate in weather like this. Who was just lying there, alone, when he ought to be getting on home. It was all so absurd.

A White Shirt

He wished he was Darrell Young, the boy who had killed Buddy. Everyone in the church, including his mother, was looking at Darrell Young as he walked down the center of the church to look at Buddy in his casket. His mother whispered to his aunt, "There's Darrell Young." And his aunt looked and said, "Bless his heart." It was like being in the movies. The only people who weren't looking at Darrell Young were Buddy's mama and daddy.

It had been like the movies when his mama told him three days ago that Buddy had been killed. Like the movies because he hadn't realized before that people Buddy's age might really die. They did in the movies, but not in real life. Because they were young. In the movies sometimes young people died to punish the wicked or because they were so good, but only old people and people you didn't know died in real life. Or some young people died in the Bible so Jesus could resurrect them again. But his mama said Buddy was dead because Darrell Young had hit him with his motorcycle and knocked him off his bicycle and he had hit his head on the pavement. And later he heard his mother tell his aunt on the phone that his father had said there was still blood on the road and a lot of people would have to pass the spot on the way to the church.

Everybody liked Buddy, who was four years older than he was. And everybody liked Darrell Young, who was two years older than Buddy. Only they said now they knew all along it was a bad idea for him and the other boys that had them to get those motorcycles, and some, like his mother, said they didn't know what a boy as young as Buddy was doing out on the road on a bicycle. Which was all he wanted to do, get out on the road on his bicycle. He knew he could ride it better if he could just get it out on the pavement. Motorcycles scared him because they were heavy. But they all felt really bad for Buddy's mama and daddy, even though they had let him get out on the road. They seemed to feel even worse for Darrell Young, even though he had the motorcycle and rode it too fast. You always thought about and talked about Darrell Young by both his names, never just Darrell.

This was the second funeral he remembered. The first one was Anna Belle Clemmer's, who he'd known because she'd baby-sat for him one summer. She died because she was fat. Being fat was like being old. So in real life fat people and old people and people you didn't know died. But now young people died too, and you knew them. What he remembered about Anna Belle's funeral was eating baked beans with bacon and three people had sung "Just a Rose Will Do," which his mama and his aunt said was just the right song for a funeral. And his father had been one of the Paul Bears, which was the people who carried the dead person. He knew Paul was in the Bible, one of the important ones just a little under Jesus, but he didn't understand how carrying a dead person made you a Paul Bear. Maybe because bears were strong.

They ate at Buddy's funeral, too, at Buddy's house yesterday, but he couldn't find the beans with bacon in them.

And then his mama had called him to her and when he got up to her chair she put her arm around him, which was something she didn't normally do. She was talking to Buddy's mama, and Buddy's mama was smiling at him. And his mama said would you like to be an Ornery Paul Bear and he said no. But his mama hadn't heard him because she was telling Buddy's mama that he didn't have a white shirt but she reckoned they could get him one by tomorrow. And then he said no again and his mama explained to Buddy's mama that he was just real upset. And then as he was walking away again, he couldn't help it, he just busted out crying.

When the funeral started Donnie Love and Allen Conner and some others all came in before the casket and all of them wearing white shirts and sat on the front row. And Donnie Love was crying really loud, but the others just drooped their heads. His mama looked down at him as if to tell him that's what Ornery Paul Bears did and he could have been one. And he was sorry he hadn't been, but he didn't have a white shirt.

Then the regular men Paul Bears carried Buddy's casket in and the men wearing suits from the Funeral Home opened it, but he couldn't see Buddy plain. And then the preacher told about how Buddy was saved during Vacation Bible School right outside the church there two years ago and how happy it made him to know Buddy was gone to glory. And then he started talking about them that weren't saved and needed to come forward and be saved before it was too late. For no man knows the hour. And he knew the preacher had talked like that before, but now it was like he was talking to him. And it all had something to do with Buddy, but he didn't know what exactly.

Then it was time for them all to get up one row at time and walk by Buddy's casket the way they'd walked by Anna Belle's. And that was when he saw Darrell Young going up and wished he was him. Then it was their turn and he followed his mother and his aunt. But when it came his turn to look at Buddy he wouldn't do it because he felt all over again like crying. And he looked at all the boys in their white shirts and especially at Donnie Love and he didn't want to be one of them. And they walked by Darrell Young on the way back to their seat and Darrell Young had tears going down both cheeks and he didn't want to be him. He didn't want to be here anymore at all. He wanted to be back at home and outside playing with his soldiers in the dirt bank next to their driveway.

But first they had to all go outside and wait while Buddy's family got seated under the tent where the grave was and then the preacher said some more words and then they could leave.

His mama told him that if he would walk straight behind her and stay off the road he didn't have to hold her hand. So he did that. At his daddy's store his mama got a Pepsi out of the drink cooler, but for the first time ever he didn't want one. His mama told his daddy again that he ought to have closed the store for the funeral and he told her again he didn't see what good it would have done.

While they were talking he went out the front door and over to the gas-pump island. This was where he knew Buddy. For Buddy came here every day to put air in his bicycle tires. And sometimes he'd come with an innertube that needed patching, and Buddy would sit and patch it while he talked to him. And two or three times some days Darrell Young would come here and pump fifty cents worth of gas into his motorcycle and he talked to him too and Darrell Young would give him the quarters to take inside to his daddy and then ride off again. Because all Darrell Young and Buddy ever did was ride up and ride off again.

He picked up the air hose and held the pin in with his thumb and let the air blow hard on his face until his mama stuck her head out the door and told him to stop before he took his breath away. He looked at the sky. It was clear with some high white puffy clouds and he thought about God up there sitting on his throne and then he thought about Buddy too and wondered where he'd be sitting up there. Anna Belle would be sitting on the porch. She always sat on the porch at the top of the steps when she was his baby-sitter. He wondered if there were bicycles and motorcycles in heaven that just ran right through each other. He saw Anna Belle sitting on the porch watching Buddy ride by on his bicycle, wearing church clothes, dark pants and shoes and a white shirt. And once again, without knowing he was going to, he bust out crying.

Ruth

The third-grade classroom sat at the north end of the school and at a right angle to all the others, so it got little sunlight morning or afternoon. The resulting darkness was the chief impression John had gathered of the third grade the year before, solely by peering through the classroom door when the second graders took their restroom breaks. In the second-grade classroom the morning sunlight stabbed the students' eyes, coming as it did through the big windows over Mrs. Brown's shoulders as she stood reading from the Bible.

Now in the darker third grade, John sat in the fourth seat, the next to the last, of the coveted row by the windows. On warm fall and spring days one person in that row would be assigned to open the windows in the morning and another to close them in the afternoon, gaining a half minute of freedom from their seats. And there were other ways in which the third grade changed school dramatically. There were new books to stack in the spaces under their desks—not just a reader and a speller, but math, language, and geography books. Every two weeks they got to check out a new library book to add to the stack as well, so there was quite a collection under each desk.

There were new classmates, too, because the third grade was the point at which they seriously began to hold students back. There were four repeaters in the third grade, but Rance Snead and Judy Griffin were the noticeable two because they were much bigger than anyone else in the class. At recess when the school year began, Rance, who seemed bigger even than John's father and had a large face under his blond and always sweaty crew cut, would pick up smaller boys like John to show how far he could throw them, so the chief activity during recess was steering clear of him. Judy, whose hair was the color of twine string and cut in layers and pushed up on her head like a woman's, kept to herself and didn't talk much, not even to the other girls. Because they were so much taller than anyone else, Rance and Judy naturally sat in the back of the room. Judy sat only one row over from John; Rance, thankfully, was all the way on the other side of the room.

Before the chill weather of late autumn set in, however, Rance and Judy became less frightening. For one thing both were favorites of the teacher, Mrs. Grace, being so familiar to her, and they each spoke to her with adult-like politeness. When the bullies from the fifth grade began to terrorize his smaller classmates, Rance came to the rescue and quickly converted the fifth graders into whiny little boys. If you accidentally stepped on his shoes in the lunch line, he would still twist your arm and make you lick the dirty spot if Mrs. Grace or one of the other teachers didn't see him in time, but at least now you had to provoke him to violence and so you stood some chance.

Judy became more talkative, though mostly with some of the boys, never really falling into one of the small and distinct circles of girls. Her classmates didn't test her friendliness too much because, like Rance, she could and still would put a twisted arm well up their backs if they happened to pick up her pen to look it over. She was one of the few in the third grade who had started using a pen instead of a pencil to get her lessons. John's own parents didn't think he was ready yet, and Mrs. Grace was not one to push the issue. For a while John was one of the boys with whom Judy was friendly. It started when one day he simply asked her if he could borrow her pen to blacken the tires on a car he was drawing and she said okay and handed it to him, acting sweet like one of his older girl cousins or younger girl aunts. He colored in the tires, conscious of how much more smoothly the pen moved across paper than a pencil. When he handed it back to her, remembering to say "Thank you," they both noticed he had gotten ink on his hands. "Uh-oh," Judy said, and she reached under her desk to pull out her purse. Some of the other girls in the class, in imitation of Judy, had begun to carry purses, too, but none of them would, as she did several times a day, pull a compact and a tube of lipstick out of theirs and begin to fix themselves right there in class. Judy's boyfriend was Eddie Joe Collins, a sixth grader, and the two of them were constantly slipping away to be together and having to be searched for and separated by the teachers. Judy made herself up just before lunch every day and again after she had eaten because Eddie Joe would contrive to be in the hallway either as the third grade passed on its way to lunch or on its way back to the classroom.

Judy rummaged in her purse until she found what she was looking for: a dry face cloth, pink and frayed. "Here," she said. She took John's hand and rubbed the cloth over the ink smudge. "This ain't working," she said. "Wait a minute. Miss Grace," she said, "may I be excused?"

Mrs. Grace looked up from the papers on her desk, frowning. "Have you finished your spelling?" she said.

"Yes, ma'am," Judy said.

"Yes, you may," Mrs. Grace said.

"Don't tell," Judy whispered to John as she rose to leave. She walked out holding the cloth balled in her fist.

When she returned, the cloth was wet, warm, and soapy, and she scrubbed the smudge from John's hand and then dried it with a paper towel she'd also brought back.

"Now you won't get in trouble," she said, and she put the cloth and the paper towel beneath her desk and began to work on her makeup. John's hand was red from where she had scrubbed it, and he was tingling all over.

But the friendliness didn't last because Judy had only contempt for anyone who got too far ahead of her in reading groups. She was always in the last, and it upset her because she was not going to be allowed to marry Eddie Joe until she made it through the sixth grade. It was John's misfortune that year to break into the first reading group, with two smart girls, a mountain boy, and a couple of sissies. The New Math introduced that year set this group apart further still, and Mrs. Grace made it worse for them by praising them profusely for helping her through the most difficult time in all her years as a teacher. After a few weeks, she selected a few students out of the New Math and gave them old arithmetics and taught them separately the old way. Some people, she said, just didn't need to keep up with the nation as much as others. Judy was one of these, and Rance as well. When John came back to his seat after reading now, Judy would look up from whatever she was doing and say, "Well, ain't you smart!"

One day as they were coming back from lunch, John saw on top of the stack of books under Judy's desk a comic book, but it was not an ordinary comic book like his *Archie* or *Superman* comics that he wasn't allowed to bring to school. Instead of an ink drawing there was a photograph on the cover, like a magazine's cover. He could see enough of it to tell that a woman's leg flesh was in the picture, and as automatically as a leaf changes directions in a crosswind, he fell out of line, went directly to Judy's desk, and boldly took the comic book out to look at it.

It was titled the *Book of Ruth*, and the woman in the photograph on the cover was more beautiful than he believed a woman could be. Her long hair was so black it seemed blue; her eyes were large and dark, and her lips red and moist like washed cherries. Her round shoulders were bare and the gauzy wrap she wore fell open to reveal almost all of one of her long firm legs. She wore bracelets and a necklace on her pretty neck, a neck that made her look breakable and helpless, though she looked strong, too, and there was a silver band around her hair. He had not thought anyone in the Bible would look like this. She was looking straight at him out of the photograph, not smiling. He did not have a word for the severe look on her face, but it was not anger. Fear maybe, but not really. And he stared and stared at her, forgetting where he was.

Until suddenly a sharp blow to his shoulder sent him crashing back into Billy White's chair, which didn't give way because Billy White was sitting in it. He cracked his elbow on the desktop as he felt the *Book of Ruth* being pulled from his hands. He sat up on the floor wincing in pain, then looked up to see Judy holding the book and looking down on him like a big angry cloud. The pain was in his head like bumblebees. And though he was ashamed for it, he couldn't help it: he started crying.

Judy's face went from blue and fierce to white and scared. "Oh, don't," she said. "I'm sorry. Don't cry. Shh. Here, you can have this if you want it."

She was holding the book down to him. He stopped crying and reached for it with his left hand; his right arm still hurt badly. Judy looked behind her quickly; then she reached down and picked him up off the floor. That was worse than crying. It would have been a 100 times better if it had been Rance. "You can have it for keeps," she said. "I don't want it anymore. Better get in your seat before Miss Grace gets here. And don't cry now."

John walked to his seat and sat down. Though his arm hurt badly and his eyes were red with pain and crying, he could only stare at the picture of the woman and wonder that anyone could be so beautiful. And now it was his.

He did his homework that evening in his room with the *Book of Ruth* on the floor beside his New Math book and his geography. He would look at the picture for minutes at a time between problems and become completely lost in the beautiful face. He had never had feelings like the feelings he was having. Not even when their neighbor Sue Belinda, who was eighteen and beautiful, let him sit beside her on the piano stool while she played "Last Date." Even though it was a Bible story, he did not let his parents see the book. And he still had done no more than turn through some of the pages inside, which were inked panel drawings just like regular comic books, only with the words in rectangles instead of bubbles.

His mother had to send him back to his room three times to restudy his spelling words for the week because he did so poorly when she tested him. She scolded him pretty hard the last time. It was not like him to be so contrary.

It was difficult to turn off the lights when it was time for bed, and when he did, he still kept seeing the face and what was below the face. Then it wasn't Ruth's face. It was Judy's. And he tingled to remember her washing his hand.

He was aware the next day of how having the book made him different. To possess something that special was a distinction he had never had before, and on the school bus, snatching occasional glances at the photograph, he thought of how he would call his friends over to his desk before the morning bell to show them what he had.

On his way into the school he passed Judy and Eddie Joe in one of their usual places, but instead of smooching and smiling at each other they were yelling. It was as scary as grownups yelling, so he hurried by.

Billy White whistled at the picture, and Baker Edison, the mountain boy in his reading group, said, "Hot diggity dog!" John was encouraged by their reactions to show the book to Rance Snead, who was in the back of the room trying to stack some round sticks at the arithmetic table.

"Hey, Rance, look."

Rance saw the book, and his eyes widened. "Damn," he said. He jerked the book from John's hands and held it up before his face. Then he pressed it hard against his crotch and made vulgar gyrations with his hips, wadding and crinkling the book.

"No, no!" John cried, trying to take the book back. But he couldn't pull it away. Watching the wrinkles forming on the slick paper hurt his heart. At last Rance just threw the book onto the arithmetic table as if to say that's what he'd do with that. John picked it up and saw immediately that the beautiful Ruth would be forever creased from the abuse Rance had given her. He hated Rance, but there was nothing he could do. He took the book back to his desk and tried to iron the cover smooth again with the side of his hand. Ruth was still beautiful, even though the creases in the slick paper made it harder work to find the lines that made her, and John was soon staring at her again, lost in his strange new reveries.

"That's too bad," Billy White said over his shoulder. "If you put it under your grammar book at the bottom of your pile it'll get those wrinkles out, but you have to leave it there a long time."

So John slid the *Book of Ruth* beneath the pile and tried to imagine what it would look like when he took it out again. He said he would not look at it again until after lunch, but Billy said he better leave it there until after recess.

Then Judy came in moving fast and hard and walked by him to her seat. She was wearing her short coat and holding her notebook and speller crushed against herself in her left arm and slinging her purse in her right hand. She sat and arranged her things noisily. John looked at her, thinking she might talk to him again, thinking if she did he might show her what Rance had done to the book. When she finally did look at him, her face was again the angry cloud he had looked up into yesterday. "What are you looking at?" she demanded. And then, because he still stared at her, she stuck out her tongue. He looked away then, and reached under his desk to feel for the book, just checking to make sure it was there.

He almost took it out again after lunch, but Billy said, "Better leave it," so he toughed it out. Then it was time to go out for recess, except for those who didn't have all the sentences on the board copied and punctuated correctly—Judy and a few others. When they lined up to go out, he looked back at Judy the way they all naturally looked back at the people who didn't get to go out for recess. He saw she was looking at him strangely, not angry and not sweet either. And he knew suddenly that she was still worried he might tell on her for knocking him down, but that was the last thing he would ever do. She just sat there holding her pen above the paper on which she was copying the sentences and staring at him. At last she looked down at the paper and started writing again.

He wished she could go out. What did it matter, copying those sentences, if she didn't have to keep up with the nation. And now maybe she wouldn't get to marry Eddie Joe even if she did get through the sixth grade.

He drank a lot of water coming in from recess, thinking that would give the book more time to become smooth again. He even got into a shoving match at the water fountain with some other boys. They broke it up just in time before Mrs. Grace came in with one of the sissy boys carrying her chair before her. They didn't have to line up now. They could just go to the restroom and get a drink of water and go directly to their seats when they were finished.

He saw that something was wrong as soon as he turned down his row toward his desk. The *Book of Ruth* was on top of the stack beneath. He hurried to his seat and snatched it out. Ruth's face was gone, blotted out with ink. Judy, with her head bowed, was *still* copying the sentences, her black ink moving across the page under her enormous hand.

The Twelfth Year

I am an ordinary man who has lived an ordinary life. And like all such men the only stories I have to tell are about men who have lived other kinds of lives. And really I have only one of those. It's the story of Jimmy Giles, at least the part of it I know.

I was walking down Center Point Road with Jimmy, just as we did nearly every summer day during our twelfth year, or during what I think of as our twelfth year, though the time I mean must have begun when we were ten and extended into our teens. Everything important where Jimmy is concerned occurred in that lump of time I remember as the year of our being twelve. I suppose all people have such a year in their lives, a vaguely bounded yet eternally fixed hole in chronological space that attracts memory.

In that year Jimmy and I marched together on terms of absolute equality—different only in the way chickens and guineas are different, with equal status in the yard and common enemies. I did not know, of course, that we were these things, did not even think about us much in words. But now I find myself having to find the words, to try to relate as exactly as I can the texture of our lives that year—a texture of dirt and sweat and barn lofts and of long hot days and fields and woods and creeks and catfish, none of which had yet become things separate from us.

I did know even then that his parents would never be invited into my house, knew it though it was never said, probably never even considered, and it was not simply that they were poor and uncouth people. My father had many poor, uncouth friends, and even though he had a good job working for Union Carbide and supplemented his good income with a small farm—beef and tobacco—he was a member of the rising middle class in material terms only. He stayed poor in his mind and habits all his life, and most of the people who came to our house were neighbors or relatives—farmers or mechanics and their wives, some of whom worked in sewing factories, most of whom worked, like my mother, at home. They were people who wore country clothes or made inept attempts at citified fashion, and some of them had bad teeth, which they showed often as they sat at the kitchen table drinking coffee and laughing over a game of Rook or Monopoly, games whose very names seem ironic comments on the lives they lived.

But this is all a bit off the point, I guess. I was trying to explain why my parents and Jimmy's parents never got together even though they lived less than a mile apart. It certainly wasn't a sore point between them. The Gileses were not social. They almost never went anywhere, together. But even if they had been social folk my father would not have had Jake Giles in his house because Jake Giles was what he was, or who he was. Character was something my father deeply believed in. "Measure from the inside," he always said. And he seemed to know exactly what he meant by that.

It was because of Jake's *insides,* I guess, that Jimmy had a life that I now think of in terms like *neglect* or *abuse*. When he came too close to Jake, especially when Jake had the afternoon redeye, Jimmy caught a good bit of abuse, by mouth and by hand; but both Jake and Sulla Mae left him alone as long as he didn't come within striking distance. Neither of them would go out of their way to find him. In fact, they spent most of their time, or seemed to, posted—Jake, with his slack and long body practically lying down in the chair on the porch beside the front door, moving only to spit tobacco juice past the porch edge, not always clearing it, and Sulla Mae just inside the kitchen door at the back of the house, looking hazy behind the screen, like a ghost woman you couldn't get a good look at, and though you never got a good look at her, you always thought she was ugly. With the one by virtue of his inertia and the other by virtue of her fixed place in the universe standing constant guard over the only two doors, Jimmy rarely went inside once he had gotten out in the mornings. I never saw much of the inside of their house. I have a habit of remembering it as a kind of medieval interior, full of dungeon gloom, but it must have been a pretty regular farmhouse, only dirtier than most. And I remember that near the back door stood a neglected slop bucket with offal dripping perpetually down its side.

It looked to us like Jimmy's folks never would die. Of course, they were only in their late thirties then, but they seemed as old as the hills they lived on, and to be washing away just as slowly. Jimmy and I spoke often and hopefully of the possibility of their dying in a fiery crash in Jake's pickup truck, but it would almost never run, and even when it did they rarely left in it together, as I said. Then there was one day as we were emptying the slop jar into the trough in the hog lot and Jimmy stopped all of a sudden and just stared at the fattest sorry sow and said, "You know, hogs'll eat *anything*, they say." Well, we never said anymore about that.

Had we lived in town, I might have been forbidden to play with Jimmy at all, but living in the country as we did, it was

Jimmy or nobody. And I think my parents believed that Jimmy was much better people than those whose loin work had given him life, although his table manners and vocabulary needed some polish to bring him up to even our plain standards. My father said many times he would never believe that Jimmy was the blood son of Jake Giles, and for a long time I didn't understand why my mother always told him to hush when he said it. She didn't have any higher opinion of Sulla Mae, and I thought she was being a hypocrite. They would express their opinions in front of me, never in front of Jimmy, of course, but neither they nor any of the other adults were as open about it as Jimmy and I were with each other. Which may be the main difference between childhood and adulthood. I have never in my ordinary adult life been close enough to another human being to wish with him for the sudden and fiery or even the slow and grinding death of his parents.

But that day as we were walking down Center Point Road we were not imagining lucky acts of providence or nature against Jake and Sulla Mae. Instead we were discussing a few points of religion.

Jimmy was saying, "Old man says he won't be fit for nothing as president 'cause he can't do nothing except what his preacher tells him to do." He wasn't quoting Jake as an authority as boys generally quote their fathers. He was just putting what Jake had said out into the world as a kind of test.

"It ain't like that," I said. My father was a Kennedy man, and I suppose I was a little defensive. But I couldn't really imagine what difference it could make to Jake what the President's religion was or even who the President was since Jake was one of those people whose lives never changed no matter what. Come lean year or fat, hell or high water, he was always in the same run-down house with the gullied hills of his few sorry acres rising up red and scraggly behind him and with a couple of sad cows and sometimes as many as two mules trying to pick their living off them.

"Well, I really didn't think he'd have to get the preacher's okay fer ever little thing," Jimmy said. "That wouldn't make no sense, and people are smart enough generally not to allow a fellar to be president who's in a bind like that. I figured the old man had that part wrong."

I said there must be some special consideration given by the Pope if a man became President of the United States.

It may sound from this conversation as though I had it over Jimmy in terms of everyday knowledge, but nothing could be further from the truth. I understood, or faked understanding, a few points of orthodoxy that he hadn't been exposed to. When it came to information picked up by direct observation and experience, he was much more worldly than I. Partly because he had an older sister, Annie Ellen, who was pretty careless around the house. At some point Annie Ellen had just evaporated, which was a little scary if you thought about it, but we didn't think about it much. And, of course, Jimmy was also smart because he had to be to avoid Jake's razor strop, beatings being the one activity for which Jake seemed capable of working up some energy. Stropping boys was a method of punishment my own father sometimes talked about as if it were an admirable part of history, but he never practiced it himself.

But there was something else, too. Jimmy *wanted* to know things more than I did, more than anyone I knew, in fact. He was the only twelve-year-old I knew who owned his own car and knew how to work on it. It was a wrecked fifty-one Chevrolet Deluxe, a green June bug. It was green anyway in the places where there was still paint. It sat up on concrete blocks behind the Gileses' house, and Jimmy worked on it all day sometimes, without help or instruction of any kind, teaching himself as he went. Because he had no money at all he couldn't get very far with the restoration, but at school he had begun to talk about automobile parts like a grown-up mechanic. He could hardly read and he made low grades in every subject, but that was because what he wanted to learn wasn't offered in school. He wanted to learn about motors, about how to make things go.

Someone had run the car off the road down an embankment and into one of the deep gullies on the Giles place and had for some reason abandoned it there. No one ever knew who the car belonged to, even though its license plates were local, and I doubt if anyone ever checked. It sat there for a few years, during which time practically everything that could be removed from it had been. The only reason the wheels and tires were not taken was that the car was wedged so tight between the two perpendicular sides of the gully that no one could get them off. It became ours, then, by virtue of that dreamy and infectious inertia of the place, and we played Fireball Robinson and Richard Petty in it almost every day.

Then one day, during that long twelfth year, Jimmy said for me to come with him, we were going to get that goddamn car. His ambition had suddenly risen that year, and he had begun to swear admirably, as if those two things naturally went together.

So we harnessed the mules and drove them out into the field where the car was. When we got there, we studied its position for a while as if this were the very first time we had ever seen it, and in a way it was.

I said, "I don't believe that car's ever going to come out of there."

Jimmy spat importantly and thought another second or two and then said, "If Dodge and Ford can just pull it out of the tight it's in, we'll go right out the lower end of this gully where it ain't deep and no trouble. Downhill all the way."

Jimmy had named the two mules himself. I never heard Jake refer to them as anything but the light one, which was Dodge, and the dark one, which was Ford.

We dug holes under the front bumper and hooked two log chains to the frame on either side. I was going to steer, so I crawled in through the same window the driver must have crawled out of the day he wrecked because there was no way to get the doors open on that day or this. Jimmy slapped the reins hard against the mules' hindquarters a few times while he whistled and shouted commands to "Get up," trying his hardest to sound mannish. The mules strained forward, swelling all their mule power against the harness for a moment so that you thought either leather or chain or mule sinew just had to snap.

It was a few seconds before the car moved at all. Then I felt it jerk hard once and stop. And then the car burst loose all at once and mules and car went down the gully so suddenly that Jimmy was pulled into the ditch between them. When I saw him go down beyond the front left fender, I hit the brake pedal hard. It was like crushing a dandelion underfoot. I cringed and braced myself for the awful thump, but then I saw Jimmy hop out of the gully on the other side. He'd hit bottom running and danced over draw bars and chains like a football player running tires and just made it out again before the car could crush him and leave me there with one dead body and all the explaining to do.

He drove the mules on then without missing a lick, laughing and hollering so hard he was doubling over, shouting things like "Ah, God, we got her" and "Hot damn, they done it. Get on, Dodge, you sorry make. Up there, Ford, you vapor-locked hussy." And then a lot of bluer things besides that. Words that usually embarrassed me, not because I was a good boy, but because I wasn't too sure what actions they indicated. Now, though, each of those words seemed somehow to indicate exactly *this* action. And I felt like Helen Keller at the pump, understanding things for the very first time, and at a whole new level.

I steered a little, but of course all the tires were flat and rotten and pretty much scraped off the wheels before we'd gone far. Then the car burst out at the shallow end and, because it was riding so low, started scraping a new road through the worn-out pasture. Any place else we'd have pushed up a big pile of loam and had to stop, but it was Jake Giles's land, and the clay just pushed up a little and fell to the side.

When we reached the grassless yard, the car scraped away the crust of clay, and in the mirror I saw chickens and guineas flurry into the wake to feast on the exposed insects and grubs. Around them the dust boiled up in a red cloud. One hen, acting just like a chicken, got caught in the front bumper momentarily and flapped crazily until she got herself loose and then went flapping several feet into the air bumping and skidding over the top of the car. She flapped through the swirling red dust and landed the bounding way harried chickens always land and immediately started pecking at the bugs and worms with the others like nothing at all had happened to her. The settling dust colored everything—the yard fowl, the house, the single and barren walnut tree, and the useless old blue and white bird dog that had been napping all my life at the back steps and had risen slowly and reluctantly when it looked like the hurtling train might crash right over him. When he saw that it wasn't going to, he stretched himself and lay down again with his chin on his paws and his big glassy eyes opened and fixed on the mules and Jimmy and the car.

And the mules, too, when Jimmy stopped them near the back door, simply stood there as if they had reached the end of just one more field in their faithful and monotonous mule lives. I was a little scared myself, feeling tight in my chest and belly the way I always did when I was doing something that would cause my parents to have a fit, but even so I was laughing as hard as Jimmy. I had to, being somehow both a spectator and a part of the spectacle.

Jimmy himself was trembling.

He unhooked the chains from the mules and led them back to the barn lot where he jerked the harness from them and threw it carelessly in a heap into the doorless tack room. Then he ran all the way back. In the meantime I had crawled out of the car, crawled out because even out of the gully the doors wouldn't open; and I saw Sulla Mae come to the kitchen door to see what the ruckus was. She stood there silently for a moment, looking all filmy behind the screen, and then she closed the kitchen door because the dust was seeping inside, as though that would have made any difference. Jimmy, who was just coming back then, watched the door close as if he was waiting for exactly that to happen.

We dug holes to get the jack under the car deep enough to raise it and slide the blocks under it. As soon as we had it up, Jimmy found a rusty wrench and sneaked into the house through a window to steal some machine oil. We didn't pay much attention to the damage we'd done, except you couldn't help but notice what had probably been the muffler and tailpipe all crumpled up in a heap and wedged against the back bumper. Jimmy went right to lubricating the oil plug, and with both of us pulling on the wrench and Jimmy trying to coax it with language, too, we loosened the plug finally and drained all the oil out into the dust. Then Jimmy drained the rusty water out of the radiator. That was probably a good idea, even though there wasn't enough of it left to make a decent puddle. This was about all he knew how to do then, I reckon, and he had to do something or die. In my ordinary life this was one of the earliest instances of something I have witnessed, heard about, and believe to be true about people whose lives are extraordinary. That there are times when life can be just too good for them to live and the only thing to do at such times is something ordinary or they'll go crazy with joy. There was the flute player I heard about who used to come so near rapture when he played that his friends gave him whiskey afterward to sober him up again.

"I'll have it running before the year's out," Jimmy predicted after he had pushed himself back from the car. He sat there on the ground, dirty and sweaty and biting the insides of his cheeks to keep from grinning, with his face looking even thinner than it usually did. A drop of sweat gathered suspensefully at the tip of his sharp, dirt-streaked nose, and I waited for it to drop, controlling my urge to reach over and knock it off with my finger. Right behind his right eye you could see a boomerang-shaped vein that was always visible but now you could see it was throbbing. I knew that he, like me, had visions of riding down the road as free as the men in the white convertible in the Wildroot commercials. All things seemed suddenly possible.

But then there was that day when we were walking down Center Point Road discussing the President-elect's religion, and we passed Mac Ferdy's farm. Old man Ferdy was stretched out in the shade of one of the several lush maples in his front yard, with one booted foot thrown over the other and his head propped against the trunk of the tree just high enough to watch the traffic passing by, which amounted to a vehicle about every five minutes, just enough to stay awake for. When Ferdy saw us, he sat up quickly and whistled and hollered, "Come over here, boys."

Ferdy told us he would pay us seventy-five cents an hour to help him put his hay in the barn. Of course we said we would. We would have done it, or at least I would have and maybe Jimmy still would have too at that time, just for being asked. Not because we were Boy Scouts or anything. Just because you didn't get asked to be a man every day.

Ferdy had mowed and raked the hay already, and it flowed out in mounded rings from the center of the field all the way to the fence in every direction. We worked for well over three hours, I guess. Neither Jimmy nor I had a watch to tell time by, and Ferdy's watch stayed the whole time deep in his overalls' pocket, buried down there like all time was his possession or something. At least that's what you guessed was at the end of the snaky twist of leather crawling down into his pocket from the loop where his overalls buttoned on the side.

We had to use pitchforks because Ferdy was the one farmer in the whole country who still didn't bale his hay, claiming you lost too much storage space when you baled it. Jimmy and I pitched the hay into the wagon while Ferdy drove it between the rows. He talked trash to the mules and stopped occasionally to pick up the fork that rode on the seat beside him and move the hay in the wagon to make room for more. Jimmy loaded on one side and I loaded on the other. We took turns working the longer outside rows, and in the barn we took turns pitching the hay out of the wagon through the opening into the loft, where the other worked with Ferdy carrying the hay back to the wall and bringing the stack ever forward. Before long our hands ached and the inexpert flesh of our arms, chest, and legs was badly scratched by the hay and stinging in our sweat. But I never lost that good feeling about doing the work, man's work, away from home, and it looked to me like Jimmy was enjoying himself that way, too. Only boys ever feel that way.

Ferdy worked hard himself, even when he was just driving, and set a brisk pace. He stopped regularly for water and more often to remove his hat and mop his brow with a red bandanna and say, "Boys, she's hot." And then put the hat back on his head and the bandanna back into his pocket like that settled that.

When we were through and the mules had been unharnessed and tied in the shade, we sat down on the lowered gate of

Ferdy's GMC while he went into the house, as he said, to count out our wages.

"We'll walk on down to the store and get us a dope and a honey bun," I said.

Jimmy nodded. "Maybe he'll drive us there." And then he said in a way that showed he'd been thinking about it, "I'm going to save me two dollars, though, to get me that used tire off of Howe. Or maybe just a dollar, and use one to get me a haircut." Sulla Mae usually gave Jimmy his haircuts at home, a process that involved a lot of head slapping and commands to "set still," and when she finished with him he always looked mangy. It took forever for his hair to grow out again to that tolerable ungroomed state he presented most of the time. "Seems like a damn fellar can't ever have enough money," Jimmy said. And I thought, "You sound like my father." But I didn't think much more about it, not just then anyway.

When Ferdy came back out he put three quarters into each of our hands.

Jimmy said, "What gives here?"

Ferdy looked surprised, but surprised like he was ready to be surprised.

"Them's your wages, " he said.

"Like hell," Jimmy said. And the old man called him an ingrate like all youngons these days, and Jimmy flung the three quarters hard against Ferdy's shoes. Ferdy jumped as if he were dodging heavy rocks. Jimmy jumped off the tailgate, spat, and walked off, shouting the kind of obscenities that even the bravest people usually mumble.

I didn't even look at Ferdy, but I got up off the tailgate. I stuck both hands in my pockets. The three quarters slid along my fingers until they fell past the tips. The last one clinked faintly as it landed against the first two, which were muffled in the cloth. I tucked the coins on down deeper as I walked away after Jimmy.

I looked back once and saw Ferdy down on his knees gathering the quarters Jimmy had thrown at him. For some reason the sight looked pitiful to me, and I couldn't stand to watch for long.

When we came to my driveway, I asked Jimmy if he wanted to go on down to the store and get a dope. It was the first thing either of us had said. He said, "No," pretty sharply, and he rolled his head at me once and kept on walking. That made me mad, or something. "Hell," I said, "there ain't no sense in coming away with nothing." He acted as though he didn't hear me. I watched him go until he turned off Center Point Road down the gravel road that led to his house. I watched him until the tip-top of his head went down out of sight, and then I turned up our driveway. I went into our kitchen where my mother was cooking supper. I almost hugged her. I knew her clothes would be damp to the touch, knew it from the days when I had clung to her waist and soaked my face in the kitchen steam they absorbed like memory. She asked where I had been, and I told her, but nothing more than where I had been. I didn't cling to my mother's waist anymore.

I passed through the kitchen and out the back door, picking up a cold tomato biscuit on the way. Inside the barn lot, I saw my father leaning backward against the barn door. He was holding his stomach with one hand and trying to latch the door behind him with the other. He had been butted by a yearling Angus he was trying to doctor for the pinkeye. I dropped the biscuit and tomato among the milkweed and clover and cow piles and ran to latch the door for him.

He took a few minutes to catch his breath and then felt his ribs until he was satisfied nothing was broken. Then he went into the stall with the calf again. He put a rope around the calf's nervous neck; and, standing in the manger, I pulled the rope until the calf's head was pressed tightly against the wall. It was easy enough then for my father to give it the injection.

I told him what had happened with Ferdy after we let the calf go. He was leaning against the side of the stall and holding his stomach. He said that Ferdy was like that and always had been. Then he said, "But I reckon boys has to learn how to deal with the old devil firsthand. Easy money and time was always his commodities." My father said things like that a lot.

But even now I have to reckon what he said is somehow true, even though things don't even out and the devil seems to have his favorites. The world never did favor Jimmy Giles. He never got that Chevrolet to run, and as far as I know it's sitting there still behind the sunken, abandoned Giles house, unless it has rusted away completely. It wasn't because of any lack of skill that Jimmy didn't get it running. Even before he was out of junior high he was cutting class to go out into the parking lot and work on the cars that belonged to the high-school boys. He failed one class early on in high school that he had to make up, but the first couple of years at least he scratched by on the whole with D's and now and then a C given by one of the softer hearts among our teachers.

But he was doomed. Eventually he became a lover of semis, and since the school was located on the highway he got into trouble often for analyzing the passing tractor-trailers instead of paying attention in class. When a teacher would call him down for this, he would frown back at her, and after a while he began to say things like, "I ain't hurting nothing" or "Why can't you just go on and leave me be?"

Gradually, almost imperceptibly, Jimmy and I drifted apart. My last real engagement with him occurred during our sophomore year, when we were in the same algebra class. Our teacher, Mr. Keebler, made his seating charts by ability. A students in the first row by the door, B students in the second, and so on. I sat in the second row, Jimmy in the last, which was okay by him because he was by the windows. Every day Mr. Keebler would send us to the blackboard one row at a time, then call out problems for us to work. The first one in each group to solve the problem got to sit back down. The problems got progressively easier, and when one row was done the next went to the board and was given a set of even easier problems to work.

Jimmy was almost always among the last to leave the board and take his seat, and he stood there most days with a couple of other boys who were so good-natured about their limitations that the rest of us would tease them a little as they struggled. Mr. Keebler wouldn't stand for too much of this kind of disorder and we were not generally cruel, but the three of them often stood there near the end of class and endured snickers and occasional comments while Mr. Keebler walked them through the steps of the very last and easiest problem before he let them sit again.

One day I happened to be the first to sit down from my row, and with this coupled with the fact that I'd made an A on my most recent test, I was sitting there pretty well swollen with pride pus by the end of class as the three struggling boys stood in inert helplessness at the board. When Mr. Keebler had to repeat for Jimmy for a third time how to write the next step in what was a pitifully easy equation to solve, I said, "Might as well give up, Mr. Keebler. Jimmy can't solve a problem unless he can hitch his mules to it."

Some of the other students laughed; I had long before told them all the story about salvaging the car. Mr. Keebler told me to hush. Jimmy himself just turned from the board to look at me, at first with a blank face, but then slowly his ears began to glow and his eyes darkened. But Mr. Keebler told the three boys to sit down. Then the bell rang.

I was standing at my locker a few minutes later feeling what in another moment would probably have been recognizable as guilt when all of a sudden something slammed into my back and I was plunged halfway inside the open locker. When I turned, there was Jimmy, staring me straight in the eye and hissing.

"Come on, you son of a bitch," he said.

"You're crazy," I said.

Then he flew into me, striking me on the shoulder. We locked arms and grappled and fell on the floor and rolled, forcing a hall full of students to make way for us. Neither of us was able to get an advantage, but I'll admit I was scared, mainly because he kept cursing at me through angry teeth all the time we held on to each other. I was certain he was trying to bite me, and I used all my strength to hold him off. We were still locked up when Mr. Isbill, the principal, who must have weighed in at 250 pounds, grabbed us both by the collars and stood us up and separated us all in the same motion.

Breathing hard and bleeding slightly, Jimmy and I sat side by side, not looking at anything but the floor, while Mr. Isbill across from us behind his desk, holding his famous paddle against his shoulder, said, "Three days or three licks," the common punishment options for any offense in his school. I took the licks, but Jimmy looked up into Mr. Isbill's face and said, "You ain't touching me."

So Jimmy was gone from school for a while, which had become the only place I ever saw him. When he returned, there were no grudges, only more distance, a final distance, between us. It was as though the fight were merely an inevitable ceremony marking, at least in parody as we rolled on the dirty school floor locked in equal combat, what we were ceasing to be only because we had once managed to be what that was: as though violence between us was somehow required, there being no formal papers to govern such matters. By the end of that year I was bumped up to the A row in Mr. Keebler's class and I became the youngest member of the All-County basketball team.

Jimmy became even more incorrigible before all authority, even to the point of refusing to go to the blackboard at all in Mr. Keebler's class. He just never learned to tolerate adults, I reckon. When the librarian, Miss Hansen, told him to bend over to receive his corporal punishment, for what offense I do not know, he told her to bend over her goddamned self. Miss Hansen had a purple fit, and Jimmy disappeared from school for weeks. Afterward he attended irregularly, never earning enough credits to graduate.

But that was all well after the long, long year when we were twelve. Jimmy Giles went on to become notorious, getting his name in the police-report column in the local paper several times and finally spending a year in prison for breaking into a pharmacy. When he was twenty-three, he destroyed himself in an automobile crash. Some people speculated on the mysterious cause of the wreck on that straight stretch of road with no other cars involved, but I have refused to, and refuse to now. I came home from college to attend his funeral. His coffin was not opened, and at the receiving of friends Jake and Sulla Mae sat dispassionately before the file of mourners, the one with a face as corrugated as his land, the other gaunt and thin-haired but not really so bad looking after all. It was hard to believe that I had ever wished some harm would come to that pitiful pair.

And afterward everyone said that it was all so inevitable. It was in the blood all along, my father said.

But none of them understood the inevitability of it all as I did; they did not know it was all the twisted coming true of an old wish. Nor did they see in it the act of the boy wild to take control of his life with an automobile that knew its most gleaming moment not in a dealership showroom or speeding down a highway but scooting through dust behind a pair of mules, bringing unexpected bounty to yard fowl and excruciating joy to young and equal hearts. They did not remember, they did not even know (Ferdy being dead by then), the boy who had flung the quarters in manly defiance, and at that same moment had pointed out the true difference that would in time emerge between our two souls. I was the only witness. And how could *I* tell them, I, who in my ordinary life would continue to pocket the quarters through the years, tucking them deeper down into the folds of the world's approval.

D & C

Caleb Vance sat in the lounge of the hospital's Short Stay Unit waiting for someone on the staff to come out and tell him his wife had returned from recovery. Actually he sat on a hard, backless seat in the hospital foyer that was adjacent to the lounge and formed with it an L around the offices and treatment rooms of the SSU. The foyer section of the L was an atrium of steel and glass, reflecting that scraped-out look of contemporary office architecture and décor.

For several minutes Caleb had been listening to the prattle of two small children and two adults—country people. One was a tall man with a dappled beard draping his blue and white checked shirt. He wore jeans and gray lumberjack socks with red rings sunk in layers over his ankles and bulging inside brown suede Hush Puppy slippers. The man kept talking to one of the two children, a little boy about four years old who kept wandering away from the adults. The man said, "Bubby, get over here. That one extra step's going to get your little hiney set on fire." The boy came back, grinning. When he came close to the man, the man winked at him.

The other adult was a fat woman with stringy black hair and glasses. She was dressed in pink pants and a white blouse and a white sweater. Her blue tennis shoes were dirty, and the flesh of her ankle bones shined like little light bulbs above her socks. Between her fat thighs stood the second child, a girl about two dressed in a bright pink sweat suit that shined against the dullness of the woman's pink pants. The child gurgled incessantly, most of the time with her thumb in her mouth, and the woman talked back to her in sweet tones and now and then wiped saliva from the child's chin with a wadded tissue she had drawn from her sweater pocket.

After a while another woman came in carrying still another child. The new woman said hello to the others then took a seat between them and Caleb. She put a heavy bag down on the seat and then stooped to pick a child's blanket off the floor. Caleb had noticed the blanket before but hadn't thought much about its being there. The new woman looked at the other one and asked, "Is this yours?"

"No," the first woman said.

"Well, I guess somebody just dropped it here then." She looked at Caleb as if she might ask if the blanket were his, out of pure politeness, but apparently she decided even politeness didn't call for anything so ridiculous, so she laid the blanket across a backless seat beside her and then put her little girl on her knee.

"She here to have tubes put in her ears?" the fat woman asked.

"To have them taken out," the new woman said.

"Taken out?" said the bearded man. He seemed completely baffled by this reversal of logic.

"She's had a lot of ear infections lately, and the doctor wants to take them out to see if that's what's causing them. They've been in there since she was three."

"How old is she now?" the fat woman asked.

"She's five and a half."

"Looks like they'd have come out on their own by now. This one's going to have them put in." The fat woman nodded toward the boy.

"Imagine that," said the new woman. "One having them in and one having them out. It's all hard to keep up with sometimes, isn't it?"

"Well, if this don't work I'm going to rent him out to some loggers," the man said. "He sounds like two chain saws a going nights."

The new woman laughed politely.

Caleb felt keenly the differences between himself and all these people. He was wearing one of his several expensive suits, expecting to go into the office later, provided his wife was okay, of course. She was in for a D & C, the first hint of female trouble. They were themselves well past the stage of infected ears. Their own son was away at school in Maryland, and though their daughter was in only the seventh grade, Caleb knew they had passed that unrecrossable bridge between childhood and adolescence, which was a matter of a change in the structure of love as much as anything else. It seemed to him suddenly that they were past a lot of things with which these very different people here in this common room were grappling.

The country family, their voices, their male angularity and female unkempt roundness, their country accents and country humor, their clothes—these were the marks of their difference; and Caleb couldn't help but wonder how they were paying for the boy's operation. Oh, they were just country people, people with bad grammar and bad personal habits who voted against their own best interests in every election because they never understood what their own best interests were.

The receptionist came to the window and stared out into the atrium. "Alts," she said, and then, "Plemmons." Satisfied she had identified the right people, she said, "You can come on back now."

The new woman rose with her child and her large bag and started immediately for the wide brown door beside the receptionist's window. The fat woman gave the little girl to the bearded man and took the boy by the hand. The man rose and gathered a cloth bag and two books—a Bible and a thick book that looked to be one of those Bible commentaries. "You want to take these?" the man asked the fat woman. She reached for the bag and said, "You hold on to those," meaning the books. The man reached down and scooped up the little girl, who was just darting away, and the woman carried the boy through the brown door. The man sat back down, thrust forward his long thin legs, threw one ankle over the other, then slipped the little girl between his legs like a piece of cloth through scissors.

For a while then Caleb forgot about these people and concentrated on why he himself was there. He felt sorry for his wife for having to go through this. Although he had discovered that apparently it was not so unusual, especially not for a woman forty-eight, the whole ordeal had put him in a peculiar mood. He found his thoughts wandering, and even more unusually and worse, sudden bursts of emotion had come upon him. It hardly seemed possible that she could be that old. Theirs had been a good life, in some ways, but he had always known that she had never been truly happy. He had known when he married her that she was deeply set in her family's country ways. They had gone to high school and then to college together and then he had gone on to graduate school, after a year of which they married. She worked at a clerical job for a drug company while he finished school, and then they moved away from both their families so he could take a job teaching accounting and finance at a small state college in North Carolina.

It was while they were there that the difference between them was made unmistakably clear, the difference that would keep them forever split in some ways. At a party at the home of his department chair, his wife had fumbled badly through conversations with several members of the faculty and their more sophisticated spouses. After one or two of these verbal embarrassments, Caleb had begun to keep his distance from her. Sometimes he would look back on that night and chastise himself. If only he had stuck by her, if only he had come between her and those damned social vultures. But he had instead denied any interest in her by remaining aloof. Toward her family and his own, toward their backwardness, their sameness in the backwardness, the nasal accents and "ain't" and "hain't" and "I seen it," he had never felt hatred exactly, just the same cold contempt one feels toward the unfortunate member of any family. Oh, Judy had not been that inept, just off guard enough to say "youns" a couple of times. And at one point during the evening, while passing an open bedroom door, Caleb had overheard Professor James Townsend saying to a couple of ladies, "Have you heard her talk about how they're trying to get the bank to *loan* them money to buy a house. To *loan* it to them. Jesus, I think if I hear it one more time I'm going to have to tell the woman the verb is *lend*; *loan* is a noun." James Townsend. Then he was a tall, forty-five-year-old bachelor whose classes were very popular among female English majors, but no one could hold anything like a two-way conversation with him. Caleb wondered if he was still alive. He hoped he was. He hoped that at that very moment Professor Emeritus James Townsend was alive somewhere suffering horrible cirrhotic pain, the bastard. The whole damned world used *loan* as a verb.

Caleb did not know if his wife ever became aware of the sport she had provided that night. She was, after all, and despite having gone to college, still a real country Daisy in those days. She had known nothing about how to estimate a sour face or a raised eyebrow. But she must have known something, for thereafter whenever they were invited to parties, always the departmental parties, never smaller, more intimate gatherings, it was she who first suggested a reason they should decline the invitation. And he always agreed. Sometimes he steeled himself against his colleagues' not-so-secret pity by his secret knowledge of her extraordinary abilities in bed, but in truer moments he had to admit that she was not so extraordinary—certainly adequate, and quick to learn and perform what she learned. But, no, not extraordinary.

Except for the holidays, when they went back to Kentucky, they spent most of that year alone in a small house they rented in an older, decaying neighborhood. Convinced that it was time to start again, the next year Caleb resigned his position, borrowed money, and entered law school. Judy worked a number of jobs to put food on the table and gave birth to their son. Things were changing.

The doors of the hospital slid open and a young woman, perhaps a girl, really, entered. She was a well-made girl, blonde, tight jeans, firm thighs, nice chest, but a face too hard for a girl, and too much made up the way country girls do to try to soften the hardness. She had either been married or had one or more steady lovers, Caleb guessed.

"Why lookie here," the bearded man said. "Told you Aunt Suzie was coming." The little girl looked up at Aunt Suzie and shrieked and struggled to escape the bearded man's scissors hold on her. The man released her, and she fell immediately into Aunt Suzie's arms.

"They already went back?" Aunt Suzie asked the bearded man as she put the little girl over her shoulder. Caleb winced at the rock-hardness of the words coming out of her firm little mouth.

"Yeah, they went back just a few minutes ago," the man said. He was rising, picking up the Bible and the book of Bible commentary, if that's what it was. "I'm going to go check on them and take these back there." The man started strolling toward the brown door, tucking the books under his arms school-girl fashion and striding like Abe Lincoln across the tile floor. He would be a shouter in church, Caleb was sure of it. In a few minutes he might have every nurse, patient, and doctor in the SSU down on their knees blessing the tubes that were about to go into the little boy's ears. Jesus, they even called him Bubba, like a bad hick joke.

Caleb was a mountain man's name.

Just as the bearded man went through the brown door a woman came out of it and immediately began looking around for something. She spied the child's blanket that the other woman had picked up off the floor and laid across the seat not far from Caleb. She came toward it, smiling at Caleb. "There it is," she said. "Got to have that. Security, you know." Caleb smiled back at her politely. For the first time he thought about that blanket for what it really was. Security, the woman had said. Caleb had thought the other woman had picked up the blanket only because someone had paid money for it. But now he believed she had picked it up because she knew something he didn't about the importance of blankets.

This new and apparently more sophisticated woman picked up the blanket and carried it with her back through the brown door. Caleb needed to go to the bathroom, but he was afraid they would come and tell him that his wife had come back from recovery. It was important, he thought, for him to be right there and ready, even though he had talked to the doctor less than an hour before and been assured that the news was all good. The doctor was a friend of theirs from church. He and Caleb served on the church treasury board together. After he had finished explaining to Caleb everything he had done to his wife and what she shouldn't do for the next day or two and then what she shouldn't do for the next week or two, he winked at Caleb and said, "You'll probably want to wait outside in the lounge. A lot of children are having tubes put in their ears this morning and it's going to be noisy back here."

Caleb had come out of the meeting room then. He had gone directly to the hospital cafeteria for a cup of coffee and then returned here to sit on this uncomfortable seat in this awfully exposed atrium and wait for them to come and tell him his wife was back from recovery. He began to realize now that he and the people he had been watching that morning were like figures on display for anyone coming into the hospital. *They*, he felt, could see the difference, all of them—the white-coated technicians and smartly dressed clerical women carrying computer programs and manuals who paused just beyond them to slide their hospital ID cards through the electronic time clock. There were also visitors who passed them to go deeper into the hospital than the SSU for some more serious business, and the weary ones who were coming out after an all-night vigil, perhaps at the bedside of a terminal case.

Soon Caleb would have to return to Kentucky to keep such a vigil at the bedside of his widowed father, whom he saw three or four times a year, a thin old man with bad teeth and a crooked back who walked one year with a cane, the next with a walker, and now was spending his last months in a nursing home being pushed around in a wheelchair by the paid hands of a stranger. What was the name of that sweet young woman he had met during his visit last spring? Margaret. Margaret had been pushing his father around and talking to him as if he were a little child. She had shown Caleb around the place. Judy hadn't come with him. Margaret took her time, as if there wasn't anything else in the world she needed to do. Women like Margaret worked to earn enough money to feed their kids, or to put their husbands through college. It suddenly struck Caleb how long it had been since last spring. Had he taken too much comfort in Margaret? Could you let a woman like Margaret do everything for you—even feel—just because she needed your money? But, no, Margaret was Margaret.

She was not like Judy, not like she was now anyway. His wife worked for a florist now, arranging flowers and hand painting vases and pen stands and paperweights. Earlier that year Caleb had looked at her while he was working on their 1040 and said, "Why the hell do you keep working? It's just more taxes."

"I work to keep up with who I am," she had said.

"Well, just who the hell are you?" Caleb had said.

He regretted saying it. There was much he wished he had not said and done over the years, or failed to say or do. He wished that he had not gotten into the seemingly unbreakable habit years ago of making himself a highball each evening and retiring to his study to read while his wife read the newspaper in the living room and their daughter went to her room to do her homework or talk to her friends on the phone. In recent years his wife had taken to brandy in the evenings, starting before dinner and drinking well into the evening, drinking into an ever deeper, profound, and grammarless silence. He wished that every Wednesday evening when his wife called their son up in Maryland that he had more to say to him than how are your classes and how is your money. He wished that their lives had not gone the way they had, but, Christ, would it have been better to have stayed up there in Kentucky and have what those people there had and what these people here this morning having tubes put into their children's ears had, and to talk the way they did? Would it have been better to have spent their lives in all that poverty, all that ignorance? Two weeks ago at church their friend the doctor who had just a littler earlier scraped out his wife's insides to make her regular again had taught a Sunday school lesson trying to make all their kind feel sorry for themselves for the way they'd lost their rural values, like it was the world's fault or something. He hadn't done it, but Caleb kept wanting to say Why don't you give up that two-hundred and seventy thousand dollar house and take your children out of that school and chuck your six-digit income and head on back to the hills?

They made him sick—people who thought roughing it meant living in a town without a mall that boasted four major department stores. There was nothing about slaughtering hogs that was good for the soul, there was nothing in ignorance that bred goodness, and there was nothing in poverty that made you independent. That was all a lot of trash. Caleb, having been one when it was still possible to really be one, knew that country people were no better than other people.

But then he thought if the people passing him and the others in this atrium now could see what was at that nursing home in Kentucky, they might be less sure of the differences. The suit, the shoes, even the posture, might not adequately conceal the past. What if someone he had known in boyhood should come through those sliding doors and recognize him?

But nothing like that was going to happen, of course. Instead the fat woman came back through the brown door smiling at Aunt Suzie and the little girl.

"He's just a having a good time waiting for them to come and get him," the fat woman said. She took the little girl, and the younger woman went through the brown door. That was odd, Caleb thought. Why would Bubba's mother stay out here while another woman went back into the SSU to be with him? But maybe the fat woman wasn't really Bubba's mother as he had assumed. That was another thing about country people, you could never be sure how old they were or how they were related. For them it wasn't a problem most of the time because they all knew each other up in those narrow, country hollows, but you might assume a man was a grandpa to his wife if you didn't know them.

The fat woman started gurgling sweetly with the little girl all over again, bouncing the child on her round thighs all the while.

Shortly, another fat woman, accompanied by a chubby little boy about ten years old, came through the hospital doors. "Looky," the woman with the little girl said. She held the little girl up to face the new fat woman and the chubby little boy. The little girl cooed, and the woman and the little boy made identical faces of mock surprise. The new fat woman was holding a plastic shopping bag toward the other woman. "Brought you some doughnuts," she said.

Suddenly a child began screaming behind the brown door, a siren-like scream that strangely reminded Caleb of the cry his cousin Teddy had made one afternoon over forty years ago when Caleb had knocked him down and gone after his teeth with a pair of hoof nippers. The little girl in pink thrust her saliva-slick hand toward the brown door. "Bubba," she said. "Bubba." She looked from one fat woman to the other. "Bubba," she said again, and she pointed again to the door.

"No, that's not Bubba, honey," the first fat woman said.

"Bubba, Bubba," the child repeated insistently.

"No, baby, that's not Bubba," the fat woman said again, and both the women laughed at the little girl.

Then the fat woman took the proffered doughnuts, just as the younger woman came out through the brown door again. The chubby little boy saw her and said, "There's Suzie." Suzie was apparently a favorite among the children.

The three women talked in a circle for a few minutes about what was going on with Bubba, but not exclusively about Bubba for Caleb heard a few details about their plans for Thanksgiving. Thanksgiving was the following week. Caleb had hardly given it a thought.

While Judy's parents still lived, Caleb's family had driven to Kentucky every year for Thanksgiving. There were forty or fifty relatives to visit over the course of three days, all seemingly jolly people who talked about nothing except people they knew and the jobs they had. They also visited with Caleb's people, but at Caleb's parents' house there was little of such jollity. There was instead a quiet and desperate wish for the visit to end. And then Caleb's mother died and then his wife's father and then his wife's mother. They hadn't been to Kentucky for the holidays in seven or eight years. Caleb wondered if the next time he saw his father the old man would know who he was.

Suddenly, the little girl broke away from the circle of women and went flying toward the brown door. The chubby boy went rolling after her. "No, Chelsea, no," he was saying. He could barely speak for laughing. "Bubba, Bubba," the little girl was screaming.

The boy caught her just at the door, which she could not have opened anyway, and turned her by her shoulders back toward the grownups. The boy's face gleamed with the excitement of familial guilt, as if they were all implicated by the little girl's mischief. Strangely, Caleb felt a wicked rush of responsibility himself, as if he participated in the scandal just because had been sitting among them so long now.

After a moment the two fat women headed for the brown door together. The chubby boy started after them, but the young woman, Suzie, who had taken the little girl and sat down, said, "No, Marvin. Can't but two be back there at a time."

"Well, Ralph's back there," Marvin protested.

"He'll be coming out soon as they get back there. Anyway, children ain't allowed."

Marvin's face fell, but it wasn't long before the bearded man came out and went directly to him and gave him a noogie. That seemed to restore the boy's disposition, and Caleb found himself mildly happy for that.

Caleb wondered why it was taking so long for them to come to tell him his wife was back from recovery, but when he looked at his watch, he saw that only forty minutes had passed. The doctor had told him it would probably be an hour. He was going to have to teach himself patience. He thought briefly of something relating to the Frazier case, took a cell phone from his inner coat pocket, and called Janet at his office to leave some instructions. He had been impatient all his life. Impatient with people and impatient with systems. He had taught himself to read French because he was too impatient to take another foreign language after finishing Latin in college. His children were like him that way. Each had been and still was an eager learner. But his impatience had cost him their love. Their indifference pained him now. Normally he didn't think about it too much, but his trip to the hospital made it necessary to think about such things. God, his little girl rarely said goodbye to him anymore when he dropped her off at school in the mornings. He thought of how only a few years ago when she got out of the car in the mornings she always said goodbye. And his son before her had gotten out of the car each morning and said, "Bye Daddy I love you." Had said it without pauses, with automatic love. His impatience had made it impossible for that automatic love to become the more mature kind of love. Patience is what he had to teach himself. He had to learn to wait for other people. He had to learn to watch things, like that blanket on the floor. Patience would have helped him to really *see* it. He had been impatient all his life and all it had ever gotten him was the habit of impatience, and money.

Try to live without it, he corrected himself. But it was harder and harder each year to keep the income up, as there were more and more lawyers in town. Driven, burning, sharp, clear-eyed men, and women too now, who advertised Wal-Mart prices as if their services were Barbie dolls or antifreeze. Patience would become a necessity; he couldn't keep up with them.

The fat woman who had brought the doughnuts came out again.

"Can I go back there now, Mama?" Marvin asked her immediately.

"No," the woman answered as she slung her purse over an ample shoulder. "We've got to get on to your eye appointment."

Marvin said nothing, then after a moment he turned to the others and cheerfully told them goodbye. The adults exchanged a few words and then as the woman and Marvin were leaving, the bearded man called after them, "Be sure and come ready to eat."

Caleb almost laughed aloud at the idea of instructing those two to prepare themselves to eat. He imagined their table, the skinny bearded man, the good-looking worn-out young woman, and several fat sisters scrunched around a table in a small, disordered kitchen, and at the head, maybe an old man, brown, grizzled, and gaunt. As the laughter rose inside Caleb it hollowed out. For the first time he felt angry with these people. Something hardened him against them.

He wasn't able to feel bitter long, for a tall woman wearing enormous glasses came swiftly through the brown door and, after first nearly passing Caleb, turned on him suddenly smiling as if she were foolish not to recognize who he was. "You're here with Mrs. Vance, aren't you?"

"Yes."

"You can come on back now."

The woman directed Caleb through a dozen or so people, parents with the children mainly, including Bubba and the fat woman, until at last she pointed to a curtained cubicle.

When Caleb entered he did not at first recognize the woman on the bed for his wife. He had expected her to be alert, practically ready to dress and leave. Nothing the doctor had said prepared him for this sight. She was asleep; one thin arm was thrown dramatically over her forehead. She was pale, and the apparition that she made suggested exposure and helplessness. Even the stubble in her armpit made him feel sick with pity.

The nurse came in behind him. "She'll be in and out for a while, but she's fine," she said. "Let me know when she wants her things. I'll check on her later."

"Okay, thank you."

Caleb moved to his wife's bedside. His nearness seemed to wake her. She opened her eyes briefly then closed them again. Weakly she said, "Hi," and she lowered her right arm until the hand lay palm upward on the bed's retaining rail. Caleb believed he knew what she wanted, and he put his own hand over hers. It was a small and cold hand. He held it. He wished things were different. He wished somebody loved her.

Camp

Justin Anderson's grades were excellent, and a strict regimen at home had instilled in the sixteen-year-old a notable discipline that distinguished him from others his age. Warren Anderson was often appalled by the lack of direction in the parenting most of his son's friends seemed to get—meals at all hours (more often than not eaten in front of the television), sleeping until noon on weekends and every summer day, floating through life with no set bedtime or curfew, without regular chores to complete before an extravagant allowance was doled out to them. No wonder so many of them had so little sense of responsibility. And as difficult as it was to be the parents who differed, his wife Lucille and he had done the job. Justin was developing into a fine young man in whom they could take pride, though there was a lot of work yet to do. The camp had been an important part of that.

Warren had discovered the camp while surfing the web and had made a thorough investigation, including an onsite visit, before sending Justin. The camp was located on two hundred acres along the Chattooga River in northeast Georgia. It had been in continuous operation for seventy-five years to give boys and girls vigorous outdoor experiences in a Christian environment, a description from the brochure important to Warren and Lucille. They were Methodists, every Sunday morning at 11:00, and the Christian element suggested safety for them more than doctrinal concerns. They had sent Justin to the camp for four years as a camper and now for the first year as a junior counselor. Someday, after all, Justin would be a man. They were confident he was being groomed for the leadership roles he was bound to assume in life, that his education was being rounded out and completed by sending him to a place where physical challenge sharpened the mind. He would learn the kind of things men had taught their sons when life was lived out of doors, but that was a bygone era (and good riddance, by and large, as far as Warren was concerned).

Preparing for camp the first time had been a deeply satisfying experience. Justin had been understandably nervous about going away from home. Lucille had actually expressed second thoughts about the whole idea.

"I don't want to hear any of that kind of talk," Warren said. Though he understood her feelings, he was firm on the point. "We've reached a milestone, and the last thing we should do is divert from the course we've followed to this point."

"But he's so young to be so far from us, and for such a long time."

"People stop being young by undergoing such experiences. Don't make a baby of him. Oh, I'm sure he'll be a little homesick for a few days, but they have far too much for him to do there for that to last long. You know that."

Though he thought the point was settled Lucille raised it again just a few nights later, this time, almost unforgivably, in the presence of Justin, as they were all working to pack his clothes and camping gear.

"Justin," his mother said, "do you really want to go to camp?"

"Yes," said Justin, "only what I'd really like would be for all of us to go."

Lucille gave Warren a significant look, but he was in no mood to meet her on this point.

"Justin," he said, "come here a minute."

The boy at twelve was not very tall. His face and limbs were round, and baby fat actually hung over his waistband.

"Son," his father said, "camp will be fun, but that's not why we're sending you. You're going to learn a lot of new things that'll be useful for you. Things besides what a smart boy like you gets in school. You're going to meet a lot of people and learn how to work with them on important tasks. You're going to learn things you'll need later on when you're a leader. And you have to start to learn these things now, because only experience can teach you what you have to learn.

"If you can understand it, son, everyone has to make the world his own. Can you understand what I'm saying?"

"Yes, sir. I guess I thought that was what the Boy Scouts was supposed to do for me."

"*Were* supposed to do for you. That just wasn't working out. Remember?"

"Yes, sir."

Warren had been unsatisfied with the scouting experience on a number of points and had finally withdrawn Justin from the program when he was inexplicably not made troop leader. But Warren's talk about the good of the camp had actually been prophetic. At the end of camp each year, Justin returned larger and more confident in mind and body, with stories of situations in which he had asserted himself and done well, especially in physical activities like swimming and rappelling. He became an expert in primitive camping, learning to construct makeshift shelters, mark trails, and read a compass. With so much buildup and anxiety beforehand, dropping Justin off at camp had been a serious ritual for the first two summers. By this time the camp was such a part of his regimen that it was hardly more involved than dropping him off at school in the morning.

But the call came early during the third and final week of camp. There had been an accident. No, Justin was not hurt, but he had been involved. Yes, it was necessary to come after him right away. In fact, Justin was in a bit of serious trouble.

Warren automatically called his lawyer, who began to make inquiries and contacts. Then Warren called his wife and they started on the three-hour drive, with only the sketchiest of details.

They arrived to discover that Justin was not actually at the camp but in the Rabun County Juvenile Detention Center. He had been arrested for assaulting another junior counselor. And a girl was dead, though it wasn't immediately clear what that sad fact had to do with the allegation.

The juvenile officer met them after a brief wait. He conducted himself as professionally as a hick in authority who doesn't want people to know he's a hick usually does:

"Your son struck a fellow counselor named Andrew Dandridge across the back of his head with a four-foot wooden oar in the camp boathouse."

"Oh, my god," Lucille said, putting her hand to her mouth.

"Dandridge was left semiconscious and bleeding," the officer continued, "while your son pursued a camper named Jennifer Wayne out of the boathouse and into the woods, where she ran to get away from him."

"Why would she be running from him?" Warren asked. "Who is Jennifer Wayne?"

"Jennifer Wayne is the deceased. At some point while she was fleeing from your son she tried to cross the river. She slipped between two large rocks, striking her head, and was carried downriver in the current. The coroner has determined that she was a drowning victim. When they were found, your son was holding on to her body on the riverbank, indicating that he might have tried to save her. He is undergoing questioning right now. I can't tell you how much longer that will take.

"There's something else," the officer said. "Have you ever seen this?" He lifted a yellow wire-bound notebook from his desk. "This was in your son's trunk." Justin's name was indeed written across the top of the front cover. Warren read through it first. It was some sort of journal Justin had been keeping.

Jenny is here again but things are not the same. When I kissed her it didn't seem like nothing to her. She just said Hi Justin, like we weren't nothing. Maybe its cause I waited so long last year to kiss her. I shouldn't have been so shy about it.

Andy is here too. A lot of the kids are here again. But I don't care about them. I just want to be with Jenny. Like it was last year. But she won't talk to me much. Saw a snake in the water today.

I kissed Jenny today. Better.

Andy got in the raft today beside Jenny before I could. I was in front of them. I turned around once and he had his hand on her leg. She let him.

There was much more written in the notebook, but this is what Warren remembered, isolated fragments that burned their way into his mind, explaining nothing. Later it would occur to him how strange it was that in reaching for some strand of normalcy he had started to take out his pen to correct his son's grammar and punctuation.

"I suggest you find a place to stay nearby and let us know where you are," the officer said when they had both looked at the notebook. "We'll call you when you can see him. He is, by the way, receiving legal counsel from the lawyer you requested."

It was seven that evening before the phone rang in their B&B and they went back to the Detention Center. They saw their son across a square table in a large room. An officer was with them the entire time. Justin was distant and distracted and did not have much to say to them. Nor they to him, for that matter. Lucille asked if he was okay and he said yes. Finally Warren took command. "Justin, we're not going to hammer at you for details now. I'm going to talk to the lawyer this evening to see what he thinks. We'll be here again in the morning, son. It's probably not the easiest place in the world to accomplish it, but try to get some rest." Lucille kissed Justin lightly on the forehead and the boy was led away again.

Robert Farnsworth, the Rabun County lawyer who took their case at the request of Warren's own lawyer back at home, called them at their B&B that evening. He'd like to see them right away, he said, and he came directly over.

"Your son will not be charged with murder," Farnsworth assured them as soon as they met.

"Of course not," Warren said. "Who ever thought of such a thing?"

"They're satisfied he intended no harm to the girl," Farnsworth continued. "And, for what it's worth, I'm convinced he didn't either. That was an accident. He is, however, being charged with aggravated assault. Thankfully that other boy didn't get a fracture and he's expected to recover."

"Thank God for that," said Lucille.

"Tell us what you know," said Warren.

"Your son caught the boy and the girl together in the boathouse. The girl was Justin's girlfriend. Or so he thought. But the other boy, apparently, was kissing the girl, and he had his hands on her, in…in a way that really upset Justin. Justin just saw red and went after the other boy with a canoe paddle. He hit him just once. That helps, too. The girl got scared and ran. Justin went after her, just to stop her; that's the key point he had to convince them of. He didn't intend her any harm. He just wanted to stop her. But before he could she fell in the river."

"Jesus."

"I'll go around and see Justin in the morning. I want to go over all this once more with him. We'll be in court for the arraignment tomorrow afternoon. I'm going to try to plead him guilty of simple assault. It'll be hard because of the paddle, but the DA might be willing. I'll know before we go to court, of course."

"What if he won't go for the simple assault?" Warren asked.

"She. The District Attorney here is a woman. If she insists on aggravated, it probably means some jail time. I still lean toward pleading guilty, though. It'll be harder to teach a jury the difference between simple and aggravated. The D.A. might go for it. She's reasonable. He only hit the guy once."

That night as they lay in the big bed in the B&B Warren said to his wife, "All this for a little fifteen-year-old slut."

"What did we miss, Warren?" Lucille pleaded.

"What do you mean?"

"Surely there was some sign of trouble. Something we could have seen. I didn't even know there was a girl."

"There wasn't a girl. Not that way. A girl like that can cause a lot of trouble in a little time," Warren explained. "We didn't miss anything. He's a good boy and will be all right about all of this yet."

"What do you mean a girl like that? We don't know anything about her. What he wrote in that notebook seems very serious. It was disturbing to read."

"Nonsense. Do you think Justin would…"

"I don't know."

"He's just a boy, for Christ's sake."

Later that night as he lay knowing he would not sleep, believing Lucille was asleep beside him, Warren suddenly remembered the only thing that might have been a sign. The magazines he had discovered in Justin's room one day as they were taking the BB gun out from under his bed. He had raised Justin violently by his shoulders until he was looking at him face to face. "You will never amount to anything using this trash. Never again. You hear me. Never let me find this filth again." He shook the boy and released him. Then he took the magazines and left the room. He had never told Lucille. It was too embarrassing. He searched Justin's room in secret for a while, but he never found anything more. He hadn't thought of the incident for quite a while.

The next day Justin pled guilty to aggravated assault and was sentenced to six months in a Georgia Corrections System Boot Camp.

The little fragments of information became clumps and the clumps themselves formed fragments of a whole, but the whole was still something Warren couldn't quite comprehend, not even as the weeks went on. Not even the visits with Justin clarified anything, for he would not tell them anything really, would only confirm what they repeated from Farnsworth, the juvenile officer, the journal they had looked over briefly and only once, or from what they guessed. Justin was changed. He was quiet, perhaps even seething, and certainly jaded. Warren complained to Lucille one evening when they returned home from a visit: "All that he worked to become—all that we worked to make him has been undone by that little slut. I don't know how we'll fix this. But, by God, we will."

"I don't think there are any camps for this," Lucille said.

"That's a pretty shitty thing to say," Warren said, and stormed off.

A few weeks later Henry Holman rang their doorbell. It was in the evening, and Holman seemed to anticipate some reluctance on Warren's part to admit him, for he was overly polite and extensive in his introduction. He was working for Peter Wayne. Mr. Wayne wanted all the facts about his daughter's unfortunate death confirmed by an independent source. "I am, as you might have guessed, the independent source."

"I suggest you go read the records, Mr. Holman."

"Well, sir, I've done that. But I could hardly take Mr. Wayne's money if that was all I did."

"Hardly."

"It would not even be right to characterize Mr. Wayne as suspicious, really. It's just that, well, as a father yourself I'm sure you can understand his desire to feel that he's done the right thing, through and through, as it were."

"Of course. Please come in."

"Thank you, Mr. Anderson. That's really very kind of you. I realize this can't be the most pleasant of times for you and Mrs. Anderson."

"No, it's hardly that. Please have a seat. Honey, this is Mr. Holman. He wants to ask us some things about the death of that Wayne girl from Justin's camp."

"Oh?"

"Yes, ma'am, you're very kind to let me take this opportunity. That's a really interesting way to put it, Mr. Anderson. That Wayne girl from Justin's camp."

"Did I get the name wrong?"

"Well, now, it's pretty clear that Justin didn't see her in such abstract terms at least."

"It was a minor infatuation at most."

"Probably. At least, that's what it would have been looked at from the distance of years. When you're inside it, especially when you're at the age that Justin and young Andrew and poor Jenny are, things like that can seem pretty big."

"Foolishness," Lucille said.

"It was all just unfortunate juvenile behavior, Holman. Wouldn't be worth a second look a week later if not for the death of that girl."

"Well that part is probably true enough. Not minding the stitches in the back of the boy's head."

"Justin would hardly have thought of her again once camp was over."

"Now that's a little harder to believe, if you'll pardon my saying. For anybody who's taken a look at that yellow book of his."

"What do you mean? We've seen the journal."

"Some pretty ardent expressions there, wouldn't you say?"

"All just kid stuff."

"Mr. Anderson, Justin uses the word *love* seven times in that little book."

"What," Warren said. He was genuinely surprised.

"Yeah, I counted. Oh, it's just the kind of thing I do. Silly, really, most of the time. I just got in the habit of detail."

"Mr. Holman," Lucille said, "was there something specific you wanted to ask us?"

"Yes, of course, I'm sorry. I've been wasting your time instead of taking care of business. Another habit of mine, I'm afraid. Just a couple of things. Has there been anything like this before in Justin's past?"

"No."

"Certainly not."

"Any other girls he had more than a casual interest in?"

"None."

"Any fights?"

"No. Justin is not a fighter."

"He ever get in trouble at school or have any trouble with the law of any kind?"

"No."

"Drugs?"

"Naturally not."

"Ever find your whiskey watered down, anything like that?"

"I don't drink," Warren said.

Holman whistled his admiration.

"So the story is essentially that Justin has always kept his nose clean. All-American kid, really. I just had that feeling, to tell you the truth. I had to ask anyway. Because, you know, I've seen a lot of things, things you just wouldn't expect from children. You wouldn't mind if anything else comes up that I just call you, would you? Won't trouble you with another visit probably."

"No, we wouldn't mind."

"And I'm sure you won't mind if I pay a call on Justin. Business, of course, but I find myself really wanting to meet him."

"Why do you need to see Justin?"

"Just business, like I say. More than anything just so I can tell Mr. Wayne I did see him when I give him the final report. You never want any loose ends. It's the quickest way to tie things up."

"One condition," Warren said.

"What's that?"

"Robert Farnsworth has to be present when you meet with Justin."

"And who is Mr. Farnsworth?"

"I'll get his number for you," Lucille said, rising.

The next evening it was Farnsworth who called.

"Warren," he said.

"Yes."

"Get here first thing in the morning."

"What's wrong?"

"Justin is confessing to killing Jenny Wayne."

It was as though the youth were not even his son—sinewy, pale from having been too much indoors, speaking with calm reserve about killing a girl. This was not his son, but another version of someone he almost knew. Warren and Robert Farnsworth were the only other two in the room. Lucille had refused to go in. And Justin Anderson was telling what had happened for the third time now, solely for the benefit of his father. Robert Farnsworth had heard it all twice before, once with Henry Holman, once with the detective from the Rabun Country Sheriff's Department.

"Jenny and me fell in love last year at camp. It took me a long time to do anything, but when I did she liked it. We wrote each other through the school year and even up to a month before the time when we would meet at camp again. Then for a month I didn't hear from her, so I wondered if she would even be at camp. But she was, and I was really glad at first.

"But it was different. She was bigger and even prettier. But she was a flirt. She would still flirt with me, but then she would flirt with other boys too. Like there wasn't any difference. But I loved her. I loved her, and I was going to make her stop being that way. I told her I loved her by the fire one night. I whispered it so none of the others would hear. And she said she loved me too, only she didn't whisper. My heart nearly broke out of my chest, but then I saw what she meant. She didn't mean what I meant. And then Andy got up and came over to me and threw his arms around me and kissed me on the cheek and said I love you, too, darling. And everybody laughed. Even her.

"The next day I saw him touch her for the first time. It was in the raft. But I didn't say anything. A few days later I saw them in the boathouse. He was touching her again. I cracked him with the first thing I could pick up. They tell me it was an oar. We both stood there looking at him a minute. He just laid there moaning. Then when I reached for her, just to take her arm, she screamed and took off. Then it was mostly like I said before. She took off through the woods then struck out across the river on some big rocks. I was just trying to catch her. I was only going to hold her and make her be quiet while I told her I really loved her and couldn't stand for her to be the way she was being. Then she fell between the rocks and down into the river. I ran along the bank watching her. She wasn't knocked out. She was trying to swim to shore. So I walked out in some waist-deep water and caught her. She held on to me. I told her I loved her and she shook her head at me. I put her under the water and held her there. Then I brought her up and told her again but she started screaming so I put her under again. I pulled her up again and told her I loved her, but this time she didn't say or do anything. I pulled her over to the bank and held her in my arms, crying and telling her I loved her. When I heard them coming I buttoned up her shorts. From where he'd been touching her and where the river had tried to take them off. Then they came and found us."

"It's not possible," Warren said to Farnsworth. "He's delusional. He just imagines it. Like some posttraumatic stress syndrome or something."

"That's possible, I suppose," Farnsworth said. "But I believe him. And so does the DA."

"She's not going to prosecute."

"Yes."

"Jesus."

"He'll convict himself."

Warren simply could not comprehend all that was happening. After a moment he was looking at the youth, only he knew it was Justin now. And Justin was staring back at him, still calmly. "You," Warren said. "You're the same. The same boy. You are a good boy. You…"

"She wouldn't love me," Justin said. "She wouldn't love me."

"So you just killed her?"

"I didn't mean to kill her. But she wouldn't love me."

"Son, that's monstrous talk. For God's sake son, you can't just make people…. Oh, for God's sake!"

Warren was surprised to find Henry Holman waiting for him outside.

"Mr. Anderson," Holman said, "Mr. Anderson, I just wanted to see you. To tell you how sorry I am for the way things developed."

"What the hell did you do to him? You made him think he did that, you son of a bitch."

"No, Mr. Anderson. I just got him to admit he did it."

"Why would he admit it to you and not the police?"

"I think it was just because I was able to get into his head a little more. See I actually believed he loved her."

"That's ridiculous."

"We think so. We never really give them credit for all they are. Then one day they show us. We always seem to forget the best love story ever told was about a couple of teenagers. Well, the plot's a little different in this case. Except for the parents. The parents still don't get it."

"If you've finished."

"I just wanted you to know one thing. I didn't go in there to get him to confess to anything. I was sorry he did it. But I did believe he did it. Because I believed he loved her. And if the police had believed it they probably could have told the bruises he'd made holding her under the water from the ones she got banging against the rocks. But they didn't believe it. They were like you, Mr. Anderson. Didn't even see the word in the little yellow book. I just went in and said the one thing I probably shouldn't have said if I wanted him to keep quiet. I said, 'I know you really loved that girl.' He was all of a sudden swelled up in tears and pretty soon had told the whole thing. After which he was all peaceful again. That's all. Well, maybe one other thing. And this is just more bad news but I feel like I should say if the boy doesn't get a prison sentence out of this I reckon Mr. Wayne will come at you with a civil suit. Probably won't happen. I expect, God bless him, that the boy will do some time."

"Shut up, Holman, and get the hell away from me."

"Okay, Mr. Anderson. I've said my say."

Warren Anderson drove away thinking not of anything Holman had said, but of Justin telling the tale he had told in calm confidence, oblivious to all it meant, all the ruin it brought to everything. It was simply impossible that there had been all along in his son everything that makes a man, and everything that undoes him.

C. K. Black

There was nothing remarkable about the way he looked as a pup, at least not beyond the usual descriptors: cute, mixed, mutt. Normal temperament. The usual annoyance of all-night yelping during the first few days of life in the half-bath off the mudroom, floor lined with newspaper, of course.

But as he grew, he began to disintegrate, to manifest all the breeds of his heritage in weird anatomical variety. His miniature head resembled a collie's, but with floppy, hound-like ears. He had a lab's short hair, though it was rust red. He had the short wormy tail of a beagle, the broad haunches of certain breeds of lap dogs, the hind legs of a Scottish terrier, and the bowed forelegs of a bulldog. From any number of perspectives he appeared to be a different breed of dog and would have given the blind men of the Sufi parable the same trouble they had with the elephant.

Of course, the question could only be considered proverbially because C. K. Black would have bitten any one of the blind men who attempted to put a hand on him. His puppyish disposition had deteriorated as his body contorted.

Richard Black often thought to himself and said to his family that he could have seen it coming. The Blacks' backyard was not fenced, and Richard spent one Saturday building an eight-by-eight pen for the dog and the next Saturday building an enormous doghouse of two-by-fours and half-inch plywood. It was so heavy that Richard found it almost impossible to move from the deck to the pen when he had finished.

All this was after the pup had several weeks' growth and the small bath and the mudroom smelled like a poorly kept kennel. The Blacks would not consider a housedog, but C. K. could not be left to roam the subdivision because of the traffic and the other dogs that did roam it. So he was penned.

"We'll have to get this dog out of this pen every day for exercise," Richard had said with conviction to his family. For three days he had walked C. K. himself, and then on the fourth day Ronnie led the dog about the yard for a couple of minutes after school before going inside to watch *Saved by the Bell*. Since then C. K. had been exercised about once a week, and sometimes entire weeks had passed without a significant break in his confinement. His world was largely that eight-by-eight pen.

Which was as much room as a kennel would afford, and C. K. was well fed and kept clean. Still Richard felt guilty whenever he heard the dog barking out back while he himself sat in his living room, remote control or newspaper in hand. He could have seen it coming, he said, the neglect and ultimately the change in the dog's disposition, modern life being what it was. Now and then, with the ache of a deeper guilt, he would realize that he should have seen it coming because the Blacks were what they were.

Sometimes Richard even theorized that the physical accentuations C. K. began to show were caused by his confinement, but that was too complicated to think through with any satisfaction. The only physical result that seemed certain to have come from C. K.'s being penned was his habit of sitting on his broad haunches with his head sunken as if his neck were threaded and screwed into the space between his shoulders, not begging, but gazing at what lay beyond his pen, exploring. He would sit that way for five minutes at a time, and the Blacks decided that he looked just like a groundhog sniffing the air.

However vague the source of C. K.'s anatomical uniqueness might have been, Richard was certain the dog's bad temper was caused by confinement. He was always playful with the family, but he took a manic disliking to anyone unfamiliar to him. He simply didn't like people. Once, early on, Richard had taken him to a kennel, intending to board him while the Blacks took a weekend vacation; but C. K. had gone berserk and bitten the keeper, a helper, and, in his excitement, even Richard himself. He'd been so vicious that Richard later told Mary Ann that if C. K. had any heft at all he'd have killed somebody. He might have anyway if Richard hadn't kicked him back into his pet taxi and brought him home again.

So it was that C. K. Black finally displayed the viciousness that his name had originally been intended to signify. "We'll call him C. K.," Richard had said. "Cat Killer." But though the dog had been named in hope, the name had been retained for a while only in irony. It all had to do with the cats.

The neighborhood was infested with them. Most were the common breed of American Shorthair whose variety of color could spasm the neighborhood eyes—black, white, orange, patched, tortoiseshell, tabby. There was one Manx that resembled a bobcat too much for Richard's comfort. Next door on one side were three cats, on the other side, two, and across the street, a dozen, perhaps fifteen. There were others whose primary residences remained an untraceable mystery and whose attraction to the Blacks' home seemed ominous and unnatural. Dried paw prints appeared on their cars overnight. Cats sunned themselves on their deck and napped on their carport. Cats hid in their red-tip hedges and crouched on top of the four-by-four post to which the birdhouse was nailed.

One morning as Mary Ann reached for her car door handle, whispering her dissatisfaction with Richard for once again leaving her window down overnight, a large yellow cat leaped from inside and fled between her legs, causing her to drop, one, her Loretta Lynn's Ranch coffee mug that her late mother had bought for her at the singer's shrine in Hurricane Mills, Tennessee, and, two, three very important documents she had brought home to prepare for her employer, Mr. Felliciano of the Felliciano and Task law firm, so he could have them first thing that morning. The mug shattered on the concrete and the coffee ruined the papers. Mary Ann put her hand over her breast and said a word she couldn't remember having said since high school.

But Mary Ann's reaction was normal, an everyday response to an everyday nuisance flaring into a burst of anger that burned itself out quickly. Richard, on the other hand, hated the cats with a nearly constant seething simmer. He had always hated cats. He had hanged cats as a boy and had never felt the least remorse for it as most men come to feel for the boyhood atrocities they never speak of as adults. Richard had sadistically bent saplings until their tops touched the ground and tied one end of a length of baling twine to the tree and the other end around a captive cat's neck and catapulted many of the devils screeching toward heaven. He'd done all this with other boys, of course, and to be fair to them all, they had heard the common stories—about cats stealing a baby's breath and forming secret societies and being the familiars of witches—so their sadism was waxed with some sense of social responsibility. Naturally they'd all stopped participating in this brutality as they grew and became more civilized and less gullible, but there lingered in Richard a vague but real suspicion of cats. He still found it difficult to pass within kicking distance of one in any state of privacy without indulging himself. He almost always managed to control the urge, but it was a kind of hell, living in that neighborhood with all those cats.

So he hadn't been too upset when Mary Ann came home one day with the little ball of red hair that would be named Cat Killer in hope, even though she hadn't consulted him about it, just picked it out of the litter their insurance woman's bitch had delivered. Just handed her a check for the six-month premium and lifted the pup out of the pasteboard box in the storage room of the Allstate office. By the time Richard got home the puppy had already established himself, a number of times, on the half-bath floor. By seven P.M. that evening he had become, irrevocably, a member of the family when Richard held him ritualistically and comically aloft before the eyes of the entire family, whose attentions were momentarily distracted from *Who Wants to Be a Millionaire?* and said: "We'll christen him C. K.—Cat Killer."

It was during a late-night downpour, about a week after C. K. had been established in his new pen and the monolithic doghouse, that Richard switched on the backyard floodlights and looked through the kitchen window and driving sheets of rain to see how the pup fared, or really to certify that he had enough sense to go into his ark once the rain started. It appeared that he'd not only gone in but had also summoned the other animals, for sitting in the doorway of the doghouse, caught in the full beam of the floodlights, was a large black and white cat.

"What in blazes?" Richard muttered, and pulling on a denim blazer and a baseball cap, he tromped through the slushy backyard to see what in blazes, muttering that he hadn't built a goddamn hotel for pets. But the cat sat nonchalantly inside the doghouse, staring back at Richard through the rain with the blue-green eyes of whatever soul lay trapped inside, perhaps a math professor, for the eyes were quizzical, wondering what the hell the man was doing out there in that weather. In the dim light that penetrated the doghouse, Richard could see the slightly larger mass beyond the cat, huddled and trembling in the corner.

Richard laughed bitterly, then turned to trudge back toward the house, stopping long enough to pick up a dead pine limb and hurl it over the fence and into the doghouse, where it clipped the cat in such a way that the cat fell, unusually, head forward out of the house and immediately bounded over the fence and into the darkness of the neighbor's yard. Richard looked into that blackness with deep contempt. Then C. K. came into the full light at the doghouse door with his happy tongue lolling and stared dopily through the rain at his master. Richard only laughed bitterly again, and thus the name Cat Killer was retained in irony.

Within the month, however, the dog's anatomy began to disintegrate and he found more than courage. In time he had to be kept on a chain whenever the Blacks got around to letting him out of the pen; otherwise he would chase the neighbor's cats onto their porches, to Richard's deep and secret delight, and tear at them madly while they perched on a porch rail or clung precariously to a door screen. C. K. attacked the cats with such viciousness that no neighbors would dare a rescue attempt on their own.

Other than a passing nod at morning or evening or an occasional exchange of weather observations on the weekends as they worked in their yards, these periodic rescues of their cats were about the only contact Richard had with his neighbors, most of whom were vague people who would probably sue a man for everything he had. When he was carrying C. K. back home on one of these occasions, Richard stroked his neck firmly and spoke soothingly to him: "You, dog, have a personality."

Personality was the only word he could think of for what the dog had that he admired.

The word registered somewhat fuzzily in Richard's mind as a way of thinking about what the dog meant to him. Always attached to that indeterminable meaning was the nagging guilt over C. K.'s restraint, which became even more excessive after the dog got nasty. Guilt combined with fear of another attempt to put the dog in a kennel moved Richard, with no way to see the shape of what he moved toward, to take C. K. along when the family visited Richard's parents in Dahlonega. The home place spread over forty acres, or speaking more historically, had dwindled to forty acres as Raymond Black had sold the largest part of his land over the years. But forty acres was certainly enough space for a small suburban dog to have a romp, and it might be that if he learned something of freedom, C. K. would be a little less nervous. Richard would even risk his losing some of the admirable cat hatred for an improved disposition toward people. He might even leave the dog behind for a time. You couldn't go through your whole life afraid you'd get sued over a mutt that, bottom line, wasn't worth much more than the collar strapped around his neck.

So Richard put C. K. in the back of the truck, under the camper top. Ronnie and Beth sat on the bench seat in the back of the extended cab and watched him through the glass. The dog sat in his groundhog's pose with his head screwed down between his shoulders and looked out the window until the truck's first lurch toppled him. During the rest of the two-hour trip he lay in a corner looking in big-eyed canine bewilderment up at the children's faces.

Richard's sister Carol and her husband Roy, who had a job as an electrician but mainly hunted, and their two teenage sons, Roy, Jr., and Donnie, were visiting that same weekend, and as soon as Ronnie opened the tailgate, Roy, Jr., reached in to pet C.

K. The dog snapped, and if the boy hadn't been somewhat tentative to begin with he might never have snatched his hand back in time. Carol wondered aloud why Richard and Mary Ann felt compelled to bring a biting dog to Mama and Daddy's, a remark that pretty much stone-faced her sister-in-law for the duration of the visit and that Richard handled the way he handled most family tension. He ignored it.

When all the others had gone into the house, Richard led C. K. on a chain across his father's pasture and into the creek bottom beyond the woods before he turned him loose. The dog began a dead run across the bottom as soon as he was free, and, after crisscrossing the field several times with wild aimlessness, he ran into the woods. Richard waited a few minutes for him to return, but then he saw C. K. exiting the woods and heading into the pasture a few hundred yards farther on. The dog stopped to eye some massive black anguses, his first cattle, who stood eyeing him back in blank animal passivity. Then C. K. took off again at a dead run. He ran up a steep hill, turned and ran back down again, then stopped for a drink from the pond, a small pond with a dog-leg that, taken altogether, resembled the southeastern United States from the eastern border of Texas to the Atlantic Ocean. C. K. stopped drinking and began running again, around the pond now, threatening on each round to plunge headlong into Florida before swerving at the last second. Richard decided it was safe enough to leave him and headed for the house.

Lunch when Amelia Black's children visited with their families was a large and active feast; and afterward they all sat around talking about the farm or the neighbors or relatives, about whom Amelia and Raymond always had an intimate, active, and up-to-date knowledge. Richard settled himself on the thick cushions of the couch and alternately napped and joined the conversation until at last he fell into a deep sleep. The women, with Mary Ann still obviously miffed at Carol's earlier remark, went into the kitchen to cook supper; and Roy, Roy, Jr., Donnie, Ronnie, and Raymond took the .22 out to do some shooting. Beth was left coloring on the living room floor, under her father's snoring.

Some time had surely passed. At first Richard wasn't sure if he had simply dreamed someone asked him where Grandpa kept the .22 shells or if it was actually...yes, it was Donnie, standing there; but what else? Out of shells. Daddy. Groundhog. Was he answering? Yes, in the drawer of the night table beside Grandma and Grandpa's bed, and yes, he was even saying the boy's name, Donnie, and something about wasting Grandpa's shells. But that all seemed long ago. Then, suddenly, Richard snapped fully awake and one sentence was clearly, almost three-dimensionally, in his head: "Daddy's going to shoot a groundhog down there in the bottom."

Richard was on his feet instantly and almost as quickly at the door, but before he could get out he heard the sharp report of the rifle. It was as if the bullet struck him, blasting something bilious from below up into his throat.

"Wait, Roy," he shouted automatically, but uselessly, as he leaped off the porch. And he knew it was useless because Roy was a crack shot if he was nothing else, and there stood Raymond and Roy, Jr., and Donnie and Ronnie all with that attitude of unspoken approval and reserved satisfaction that comes over the hunting party after a kill.

"What's a wrong?" Raymond shouted back over his shoulder.

But Richard was headed for the pasture gate at a dead run and could barely be heard when he said, "Damn it, Roy probably shot my dog."

And Roy had. Right in the head. C. K. lay in a corner of the pasture at the edge of the woods, where he had gone into the fatal pose, his head all but floating in the blood pouring out the exit wound. Of course there was nothing to be done, not even anything to be said except for the unpleasant and all but perfunctory business of articulating over and over again the accidental nature of it all, and even that had been exhausted before the men reached the spot. So the men and the boys stood over the dog in a strange silence, forming a tableau of solemnity. It was business as usual, though, when they buried C. K. in the woods. "Better hone that shovel and axe to cut through the roots," Raymond said.

It was only at supper, when they were eating, with hardly diminished appetites, the warmed-over ham from lunch with freshly cooked vegetables, that Roy began to say the obvious things again. "I swear he looked just like a groundhog. I could have told with binoculars or a scope. But I never seen a dog set hardly like that anyway. I ain't never made a mistake like that, dern it." None of it brought any comfort, even to Roy. Finally, Mary Ann said, "Well, I guess the vicious thing won't go anywhere else with us." And while on the surface what she said was even more ridiculously obvious than Roy's meandering defense, it settled a score with her sister-in-law and brought some comfort to Richard. At least now he wouldn't have to worry about some neighbor suing him for everything he had.

After supper Raymond, Roy, and Richard went into the downstairs den where Roy kept the Jim Beam. It was their custom to have a couple of drinks together, talk a bit more than they did when they weren't drinking, then stagger back upstairs weary with whiskey and visiting for the eleven o'clock news before going to bed. Tonight, though, both Roy and Richard poured themselves a third drink and then started a fourth, and still they talked stiffly. At 11:00 Raymond started to put the bourbon away to go back upstairs, but both the others said to leave it. And they kept on drinking. Richard turned on the small television his father sometimes watched down there, and he and Roy watched kick boxing for a while, then monster truck racing, still not saying much, silently sipping their drinks.

At last Richard fell asleep in his chair and when he woke Roy was gone. Women were wrestling on television. He switched off the set and thought about trying to make it up the stairs to bed, but he decided instead to lie down on the sofa. He pulled one of the three Afghans on the couch over him, thought about what happened to C. K. momentarily, then slipped into sleep.

Later, for the second time that day, he snapped suddenly awake, but this time to discover that he was already on his feet. He'd been sleepwalking, and he was holding a length of firewood in his hand. He broke into cold sweat as he remembered that in the nightmare he had been trying to find a panther that had somehow gotten into the house.

Richard Black's Romance

My belly is a dead catfish, Richard Black was thinking. He was looking at it, sagging over his belt and even part of his lap, as he rocked on his front porch half reading the newspaper and half minding his daughter Beth who was playing in the green turtle-shaped sandbox he had bought for her the day after he got laid off from the Mushroom Plant.

When had he started to get so fat? He couldn't remember. But he remembered a firm, tanned stomach where now there was this white wad like the underbelly of a big catfish pulled out of Carter's Lake. He remembered the time when Mary Ann commented regularly on how flat his belly was.

But that was a long time ago, maybe; it was hard to know if it was long ago or not so long ago. And sometimes he wished she'd just come right out and say he was fat now instead of politely ignoring the fact, the way you ignore someone's disease in front of them. Fat and unemployed. That was him. The word *love* came into his head. It had more and more lately, and the fact had been a cause for wonder to him. He grabbed a handful of his belly flesh and in disgust said, "Shit."

The little girl heard him and stopped shoveling sand. "Wah, Daddy?"

"That's all right, baby."

At the beginning of April the pink slip (which wasn't pink) had come with his paycheck, out of which he had bought the green turtle sandbox, but it wasn't a surprise. He had already been told in so many words by Little Jimmy DeMure. "What this means is some people's butts will get canned," Little Jimmy had said, holding up the memo. "There's a lot of jargon about 'renovation policy' on this here, but that's what it all boils down to. I been with the company long enough to know that."

There was no reason to doubt what Little Jimmy said, and while Richard was not as young as some of the other workers at the plant, he had no more time in than most of them there. It was hard to think the words printed under the familiar logo of the parent company—a squarish human figure surrounded by stick-like suggestions of crops and refineries—could have anything like that meaning in them. It was the same logo that appeared on the paycheck that he had been collecting every Friday for two years without giving much thought to its source. He could no more have given the name of the person who signed his checks without looking than he could say whose picture was on a thousand-dollar bill. But as he finished eating his honey bun (they were in the break room when Little Jimmy interpreted the memo for them), it came to him that those words on the memo which he and most of the people he worked with would have had a struggle to comprehend (and which they weren't even supposed to see and would not have seen if not for Little Jimmy) had been thought up by a man that he would never in his life lay eyes on. And that man would never lay eyes on him, or care to, but had sent those words down on him sure and thoughtless as lightening.

Richard choked on the last bite of the honey bun. This was his third job in ten years. The first two were construction jobs he had left because they were undependable. This job had seemed as solid as the forklift he drove, and now it was evaporating like a wet weather spring in late August. Little Jimmy was the countrified voice of the world, and it was saying that everything was mist. Richard was thirty-one years old and had twenty-eight and a half years to pay on the mortgage and two maxed major credit cards. So the day after he got laid off he went to Wal-Mart to buy oil and filters for his truck and while he was there he bought the green turtle sandbox, because it came in a large box. He also bought a baseball card album and one hundred baseball cards for his son Ronnie.

It was not so bad after a few days. A kind of innate discipline seemed to be awakened in him by unemployment. Some men might sit around in their underwear all day or start drinking before noon, but anybody with a brain ought to be able to organize a day to get some use out of it. Hell, his father, who had left the farm to work for Union Carbide, had still lived his entire life as though it ran by some internal clock rather than the company's. A man could do that still, surely.

Each morning Richard got Ronnie out of bed and made his breakfast while Mary Ann got ready for work. Then he woke Beth and dressed her. She was still just a little bundle of sleepiness when he buckled her into the seat beside him. The three of them left the house in Richard's pickup at the same time Mary Ann drove off to work in her Skylark. After dropping Ronnie at school, Richard took Beth to the Sweet Tots Daycare Center where she had her breakfast with the other children at a long, low table, maybe a dozen in all, black and white, one little Iranian boy, one little Indian girl. To Richard they looked like rows of the hen eggs he used to collect for his mother from the nests in the yard and barn back home. He came home then and poured himself a cup of coffee and sat down in the living room for two hours to watch the second half of *Today* and then *The View*. He felt brighter after a few days of watching these shows each morning. He felt more informed. There was a more deadening effect to starting each day on a forklift than he had realized. But two or three times he felt a little silly when he spoke aloud to respond to someone on the television. He was becoming like his Aunt Louise, whom he had laughed at for years for screaming obscenities at professional wrestlers on TV.

It was hard to leave the TV after *Montel*, but he had to draw the line somewhere, so at eleven each morning he went into his workshop. Family members and old neighbors (the Blacks had little to do with the new neighbors in the subdivision) were giving him projects—bookshelves to build, picture frames to mend, and similar jobs—and he had some projects of his own. He had built garden benches to set around the ever-widening vegetable and flower garden that was slowly replacing the ordinary and weedy backyard they had found when they moved in. He made things for inside the house, too: napkin rings, napkin frames, a magazine rack, a spice rack, a gun case (too expensive), some wooden toys for the children (a duck for Beth and a truck for Ronnie), which he had left in their rooms instead of making an occasion out of presenting.

He'd get hungry around twelve-thirty and make himself a sandwich to eat while he watched a fix-it lady on TV do repairs around her house. He didn't learn much from her; she seemed to be trying to teach *women* about things, but he liked her because she was sweet and funny and didn't mind being a woman and she was good-looking and friendly, sexy in a way. Sometimes he'd watch the aerobic workout program that came on immediately afterward with its very different women—sleek women working out in their spandex suits—but he always felt a little depressed after he had watched them for a while.

He'd go to the mailbox then, but there was never anything interesting in it for him except maybe near his birthday. One afternoon it occurred to Richard that if ten years ago he had started writing letters to people he knew well but no longer saw, people he had gone to school with and worked with, and if those people had written back, by now he'd probably be getting and writing a letter a day. It ordinarily seemed he didn't know anybody, but there really must have been hundreds if he just started counting. For a minute he didn't see how he could possibly write a letter a day, even if he learned how to use e-mail, but his brain was still working on the old time, the time of employment; and he laughed when he realized he was still thinking that way. It was something like feeling pain where a severed limb had been, he guessed, or still feeling your cap on your head long after you've taken it off. He puzzled for a while over which it was more like, but he couldn't decide finally.

At two-thirty he left home to pick up the kids. This was not a burden, but one of the highlights in Richard's day. He drove to pick up Ronnie first, always arriving earlier than necessary to get a good parking space. Which did not mean a spot near the front of the line. Instead he parked in a lot adjacent to the driveway most of the parents used to pick up their kids. He liked being detached and watching the proceedings, especially the mothers who got out of their cars and gathered in several groups to talk each afternoon. Some wearing sweats; others their secretaries' or insurance salesperson's dresses; others jeans; and one quite often arrived in a red and white tennis dress, daringly short even if the panties were the kind it was okay to see, and her long brown legs were so attractive down to where they disappeared in the ugly knobs of her rolled-down sweat socks that he wondered if she really just put that outfit on to make the other women envious. But there was not an unattractive woman among them; some were darkly Hispanic and some were richly black and some were tanned and some were as white as down. Richard began to realize how rare ugly women were these days. In his childhood and youth they had seemed plentiful.

Not long before the bell rang each day the smart-looking woman principal came outside to watch over the afternoon departure. She smiled and spoke to everyone, and her short hair defied the wind. Richard wondered what she was like at home. And he wondered what it would be like if maybe he had gone to college and met her there and they had fallen in love and gotten married and now she had this very steady job and he was doing…something.

After returning home with the kids, he would drag the wooden rocking chair given to him by his grandmother out of the living room and onto the high front porch to sit and read the *Journal*. It was a long, covered front porch, a rarity in modern houses and a feature he relished. In front of it the previous owners had set out red tips that had grown to the height of the porch rails. They were bordered at the sides and along the front by railroad ties. The whole effect was dark and rustic, but a bit bloodied when the sun infused the top leaves of the plants early in the afternoon.

As Richard read the paper, Ronnie milled about vaguely inside the house making noise enough for signs of life and Beth sat for two hours or more playing in the sandbox. Richard began smoking again—cigars rather than cigarettes, though, thinking he'd smoke fewer and not inhale as much, and only in the afternoon while sitting on the porch with his newspaper.

The afternoons soon took their routine shape as he smoked two or three cheap cigars, rocked erratically, and struggled with the large pages of the newspaper. Occasionally he looked over the top of his paper and the tops of the red tips to verify Beth and listened for noises inside the house to verify Ronnie. The only real interruption of the routine occurred after four-thirty two or three times a week when the people who lived directly across the street had pizza delivered and a little white Hyundai whose engine sounded like four marbles rattling inside a Crisco can came ripping up the dead-end street and then without slowing in any perceptible way whipped violently into the neighbors' steeply inclined driveway and then stopped near the top of the hill as abruptly as if you'd hit the pause button on the VCR. And there seemed to be no interval between the car's stopping and the kid's getting out, carrying what looked like a stadium cushion. It was always the same kid, a tall, skinny, pale boy who looked ridiculous in the red and blue uniform. Certainly not a kid you would ever see in one of the pizza company's commercials, with that long greasy blond hair hanging out from under that red, white, and blue cap and a face riddled with acne that you could see even from across the street.

The kid always stopped the Hyundai just before it topped the rise of the driveway, always left the door open, always bounded to the front porch in eight steps, then always bounded up on to the porch in three, and always quick-stepped down the porch steps again, and always trotted back to the Hyundai with his hair bouncing against the back of skinny white neck; and his arms on the way back were always held high against his sides so that he looked like a harried chicken.

That boy had a job.

And in some ways he reminded Richard of himself, though not in the particular mannerisms, and certainly there had been nothing like pizza delivery when and where Richard had grown up.

Then Richard would look at the want ads. It was interesting to read about some of the jobs he wasn't qualified for. There were a lot of technical positions, many he didn't understand the titles of, like Technical Support Engineer, Systems Analyst, and Data Administrator. They made him think of the white-coated technicians at the Mushroom Plant who were always plunging meters into the trays of mushroom soil and congregating to discuss their readings. They had always seemed funny to Richard, meeting like that to figure out how much water or nitrogen there was in the high-grade manure (the word was that the company used the manure of thoroughbred horses only, shipped down in trucks from Kentucky). But the white-coats seemed to think all that was very important. They might have been building a new nuclear weapon or a Star Wars missile defense system for all the way they acted. And they were awful snobs. They wouldn't even nod at the men on the line. Richard often had a good view of them from his forklift. They didn't seem to see any difference between the men and the machinery. Even their bosses—even those in ties and jackets who came in from time to time to look things over—passed the time of day with the workers on the line, but not these white-coats. Maybe they weren't snobs, though. Maybe they were really just as serious as death about the moisture content and nitrogen level of high-grade horse shit.

If a college education made you so you couldn't tell a pile of shit when you saw it, Richard couldn't see any advantage in pushing Ronnie and Beth in that direction and making them unfit for a practical life. Mary Ann, though, was always worrying about saving money to send the kids to college and always telling him how much it was supposed to cost by the time each one of them was old enough to go. Richard always forgot how much she said it would be. Her worrying about such things was the reason she worked so late and most evenings even brought home extra work to do for one of her bosses. He would listen to the rapid clicking of the computer keyboard in the evenings as she worked in the back room she called the study. There was something thrilling about the swiftness with which she could fill up a blank screen. But that was the way she went about everything in life, filling it up by rapid little increments of activity, all done in preparation for the certain future she saw, all done toward some goal, though it looked like she was just filling up time if you didn't know her. She was like the pizza delivery boy, too, in her swiftness. And like the white-coats, too, in her seriousness. And even if he did know her, parts of her life put her in that world that seemed more and more foreign to him now, which was a strange thought for a man of thirty-one to have about his wife, or the world.

About three times since he had lost his job Richard had overheard Mary Ann filling up time crying in the bathroom, her sobs filtering through the bathroom door in a slow beat. Each time he had walked away from the bathroom door without saying anything to her. He wouldn't have known what to say.

He was telling himself that in a few days he would seriously get about finding a job, but he knew he was feeling something a man couldn't feel when he had a job to go to every day. He guessed you would call it freedom, but it wasn't exactly freedom. It didn't have anything to do with the freedom you thought about when you pledged your allegiance, for example. It was vague, and far from pure, for there was a good deal of guilt mixed up in it.

Still, he spent a lot of his time just remembering things in a cigar-smoke haze and with his paper lying loosely between his fingers, remembering mostly seemingly meaningless details from his childhood. Then these memories would play themselves out, and Richard would be startled to find himself sitting on his own front porch in the now. Beth's turtle sandbox sat in the dappled shade of a drooping willow beside the driveway. The willow had dropped its pods that looked like wooly worms and put on its leaves, and its newly heavy limbs shrouded Beth's play area. The grass had recently greened; Mary Ann's daffodils bloomed in clumps not far from the sandbox; and the sun shined over the house from behind, throwing shadows toward the cul-de-sac. Richard looked over the top of his paper, which he wasn't reading because he had been remembering, to verify Beth, and for only a second, just long enough to make his heart hurt, he saw something else. Or thought he did, but he really couldn't have, for as he saw clearly after that first part of a second, there was nothing there but his daughter and the rest of the usual scene. He could not even recall what it was that he thought he had seen, whether it was something dangerous or fleeting, some beast or bird, some stalker or dodger. He only felt vaguely that he had seen something and he began to look at his daughter to assure himself that the phantom, if that was the right word, was only a trick of his mind. He was suddenly and unexpectedly so overcome by his feelings for her that he whimpered a little cry of pain, loud enough for her to hear.

She whipped her head at him and, smiling accusingly, mockingly, said in four-year-old adultness, "Daddy, did you burp? What are you supposed to say?"

"Excuse me," Richard managed to reply, despite the restriction in his chest. What on earth could he ever do for her?

He needed to get up right then and go look for a job, but he feared making the rocking chair teeter over if he moved. Even as he felt it, he knew it was ridiculous, and he almost laughed at himself sitting there frozen with nerves iced over in the storm of contradictions. His acute anxiety ended only with the familiar distraction across the street of the little pizza Hyundai and the pale, blond delivery boy.

The next day Richard picked up his unemployment check and then drove straight to Ronnie's school, even though it was an hour before school let out, and for forty minutes or more he just sat in the daylight emptiness waiting until the mothers began to arrive. But somehow things were still empty even then. He took the kids to Baskin Robbins after picking them up. Ronnie didn't know quite how to react to this windfall, and he ate his chocolate cone quietly. Beth, however, made a mess of herself with her sundae, and Ronnie stared in apparent disbelief at his father, who only laughed at her. And then, on another afternoon, when Richard took them to the park to go fishing, Ronnie sat quietly for a full half-hour before he cracked the first laugh. But he finally did, and caught a fish besides. Beth caught two—small bream, her very first fish. She was puzzled by the whole process and a little frightened of the fish, and her smiles were cautious and strained. Richard and Ronnie laughed at her.

The kids began to meet their mother at the door screaming at her what they had done that day after school. Overwhelmed, Mary Ann usually said, "Please, I just came through the door." Richard wished there was some way to tell her what life was really all about, but every explanation which had sounded perfectly logical a few hours earlier melted like foolish snow in her industrious gaze as she stepped through the door carrying whatever bundle of work she had brought home to do that evening after the children had gone to bed.

He did, at last, talk her into taking a day off. That morning he told her to stay in bed, and he got the kids ready and took them to school. When he came home again, he undressed and got into bed with her and they made love. After a little while they showered together, and when they came out she started to dress. He took her by the wrists and pulled her onto the bed with him. She resisted at first, protesting that she was going to start a load of wash, but he said, "Girl, don't you know what a day off is for?" She collapsed on the bed, laughing. He held her for a long time; then they both fell asleep. When he awoke, he began to make love to her again. At first she jerked, as if what he was doing hurt her, but then she settled into the motion. Afterward they lay apart, dozing, but now and then he would reach for her and when he touched her she would move and smile. It was like being with a completely different woman. No, it was like being with the woman he was supposed to have been with all along.

They stayed in bed all morning. Richard got up at noon long enough to make some coffee and sandwiches for them, which they ate while laughing at a soap opera on television. They made love again, and then they just lay for almost two hours doing nothing but dozing and touching each other. This was what Richard had longed for, this illustration of reality which he could never have explained to her. This was the island life they should have had—the two of them, the four of them—for it was all too evident to him now that the life he had lived before was all wrong. It was all muck.

At 3:01 he left to pick up the kids, who were only mildly disappointed to learn that they were going straight home. "You need to spend some of your mother's day off with her," Richard told them. Later, he was smoking his cigar and holding the newspaper, though he was not actively reading it, in the rocking chair on the front porch. Beth was playing in her sandbox and Ronnie was in the house with his mother. It was nearing suppertime, and Richard was keenly aware of his hunger, something he had not been much aware of lately, he realized. He was made even more aware of his hunger by the arrival of the little pizza Hyundai making its delivery across the street. The regular boy hopped out with his insulated pizza. How in God's name could anybody eat that much pizza?

As if she was in tune with what he was thinking, a thought that made Richard smile, Mary Ann came onto the front porch then to ask him what he wanted for supper, but before she could finish, Richard was distracted. A sound had caught his attention. At least it registered as a sound, a vague but meaningful click, though even a second later he couldn't recreate what he thought he had heard. His first thought was to check on Beth, who was purposefully scraping sand with the side of her hand. Then he saw what it had been; the Huyndai was rolling backward down the neighbor's driveway. Its door was open, and the pale kid was not inside.

When he landed, after leaping over the porch rail and the red tips, he heard the snap in his right leg and thought *broke*. But already it was like something he had known yesterday. Even the fears that preceded the breaking of the bone had passed, the sudden fear of falling as he looked down and saw the ground rising after he leapt, after the initial fear had pulled him irrationally over the rail upward and outward. The only practical effect of it all was that his damn right leg was reluctant to follow where each new fear led. And that was strange too, how each second had its original fear that replaced the previous one the way the letters followed one another across the screen when Mary Ann typed rapidly. He felt time shatter, felt it shattering. It was taking forever, but there was not enough time for all. He hopped, finally, on the left leg, letting the right dangle and bounce wherever it had a mind to.

He was watching the car coming, thinking: *It will turn when it hits the curb.* But the curb was too smoothly formed to affect the Hyundai's direction or its speed. Beth was still scraping sand into the ridges with the side of her hand. He screamed her name. The ridge of sand beneath her hand disintegrated as she flung her hand away from it. She made a sound, but her face wrinkled like a puzzle as Richard leaped in small bounds toward her. Richard plunged headfirst then, hearing his own name screamed obscurely behind him as he did. Mary Ann, he thought, as he felt his fingernails dig into the flesh on the back of Beth's neck. He was grappling for her shirt collar. Trusting that he wouldn't miss and mad that he might. He remembered to tuck his right arm under his body as he fell and rolled. He saw Beth fly over him, extended on his arm like a car on the mechanical arm of a carnival ride. Only then did he know he had her. Over and down, landing on the concrete driveway, her body moved without resistance or propulsion, without any indication that it was living flesh.

He rolled on top of her and arched his back against the impact he expected, thinking *maybe it can't get all the way through me to her*. Then at his back he heard the splitting of the plastic turtle sandbox. The Hyundai was rolling through it with both the right rear and the right front tires, and then the car thumped repeatedly as if it was rolling on bad shocks as it went on, passing close enough for Richard to feel the breath of its exhaust. It bounded on across the yard until it was stopped by the railroad-tie border that fronted the red tips.

Beth began crying, and Richard could feel the spasms in her tiny body. He enveloped her tighter, scrunched her between his thighs and his chin. He saw that her forehead was bloodied and he almost cried at the sight. "Shh, shh," he whispered. His mouth lay directly over her ear. It was like whispering into a thimble. He raised his head then and looked at his broken leg. It was only a broken leg. Beyond it the Hyundai was pressing mildly and uselessly against the railroad tie. When he turned to look at Beth again, he saw the pale blond kid running away down the street. He had lost his hat, and his long hair flew back from his shoulders in the wind of his hysterical flight. Run, Richard thought, run. And then Mary Ann was there, touching him.

Two hundred and fifty thousand dollars. That was the amount of the offer from the pizza company's insurance. All he had to do was sign the letter stating that this settled everything and the company would be not responsible for any future claims for damages. Richard put the letter, unsigned, with one of his own in an envelope and mailed it back to them. In his letter he included an itemized bill for medical expenses that had not been paid by their own insurance, the sandbox, and an estimated labor charge for repairing the damage done to his yard and shrubbery.

All tolled it came to $8,002.36. Richard wrote, "My wife's boss, who is also a lawyer, says that this is not the way for us to handle this. He says you won't pay any money unless we sign the letter that I'm returning to you here. He says you can't afford to admit any kind of fault unless you can close the matter at the same time. I thought about your predicament and believe I see it. But what I finally think is that just because a man is not liable to do the right thing is no reason not to give him the opportunity. If you pay me $250,000.00 and I sign this letter I'm just a claim settlement. If you pay me $8,002.36, then right is done and I'm still me. That should make plain to you why I prefer to do business this way. You'll be glad to know that my little girl has healed up very nicely. She did not have a concussion, as we were so afraid she would, and the scar above her eye will fade out in time, the doctor says. The orthopedist says my cast can come off in about three more weeks. It was a clean break and he doesn't expect any kind of complications.

"When I look back over what I wrote, I'm afraid I sounded uppity in that part about giving a man a chance to do the right thing. I didn't mean to suggest you weren't a good man. I've just had a lot of time to think about things like that lately and at the risk of sounding even more uppity I'll pass along a couple of things I think I've learned. I've learned that you can't put your baby in a sandbox and expect her to be safe from the world and that it's probably not a good idea to spend too much of your time sitting on too high a porch.

"My insurance company has paid for the medical expenses beyond what I include in the amount stated above, and they might want to settle with you on that. But if you have to do something with the balance of the money, I'd suggest you put it into a driver's training school for pizza delivery boys. You might not have caught that boy that delivered in my neighborhood. He was still going pretty fast last time I saw him. But I can see how something like that might be a real benefit for others.

Sincerely, Richard Black."